The Non-Disclosure
Agreement

Kelsey McKnight

The Non-Disclosure Agreement

Limitless Publishing, LLC
Kailua, HI 96734
www.limitlesspublishing.com

Formatting: Limitless Publishing

ISBN-13: 978-1-64034-079-4
ISBN-10: 1-64034-079-3

Chapter One

Holly took in a deep breath of city air as she locked her apartment door behind her. She triple-checked the knob before following the map on her phone toward the subway station. She had never been in such a densely populated space before and found she was too timid to shove and fight, to be the first into the cars. When she finally thrust herself inside, she was able to take stock of her new life and prepare herself for the day ahead.

She had borrowed a few professional pieces from her mother's closet to wear until she was able to replace them with new versions after her first paycheck. A carefully selected gray skirt, a white blouse that buttoned to the neck, and a gray suit jacket that matched the skirt perfectly gave Holly the feeling of corporate America. She debated wearing a pair of cute high heels that she'd bought for a friend's wedding a few years back, but instead went with a pair of flat slip-ons that would be perfect for pounding the pavement and running to the nearest coffee shop to get her new boss a latte, just like in the movies.

She'd twisted her hair into a sensible bun and applied minimal makeup to complete her no-nonsense look. While other women might have gone for style over comfort, Holly was not about to let a pair of cute shoes stop her from being able to do her duties. Besides, she wanted to be taken seriously and was afraid no one would respect a shy, petite blonde in high heels in the big city.

Three scary subway trains, a few wrong turns, and six blocks later, Holly made it to the Cantrell International office building right on time. It was a monstrous seventy stories of reflective steel and glass, looming so high Holly almost feared irrationally that it might topple over. She straightened her knee-length skirt and opened a pair of giant doors that led into the main lobby. Dozens of people filed noiselessly in and out of elevator doors, never speaking to each other. The silence was only broken by the sharp *tap-tap-tap* of women's high-heeled shoes on the shiny white tiles. As she looked around at the sleek city women with their perfectly tailored suits, flawless makeup, and pointy stilettos, Holly suddenly felt like a dowdy pigeon that had wandered into a nest of tropical birds.

She stepped over to the security desk and dropped her license and proof of employment in front of the guard. Her hands were sweaty and she kept glancing nervously around the busy lobby. Everyone seemed to be in such a hurry. "Excuse me, sir, but I believe you have a badge for me? My name is Holly McIntyre and I just moved here from

Michigan to work for Mr. Cantrell. I've never been to New York City and—"

"Here's your card, sweetheart," the guard said in a thick Brooklyn accent, slapping a piece of plastic down on the desk. "And a word of advice? Don't talk so much. You need to be tough to make it in this building."

Holly nodded and meekly slid the ID off the counter before turning toward the elevators. She felt her cheeks burn with embarrassment and internally abashed herself for rambling to a perfect stranger. She was used to chatting with everyone back in Michigan and now she'd just made herself look like a fool to the first person she met in the building. What a great way to start to her first day.

The elevators were packed, going up, and Holly had to squeeze herself between two very large men carrying briefcases to make her way up to the top floor. As people left the lift to exit to their levels, Holly gave herself a short, meaningful pep talk to fill the time during the long ride up.

Okay, Holly, you can do this. You can make it through this. This is just a building in a city, not one of the most major companies on the East Coast for marketing and international sales. So what if it controls eighty percent of the sales to China? All you'll be doing it fetching coffee and picking up dry-cleaning. No big deal! Maybe you'll address envelopes sometimes or water plants. Totally doable! Fake it until you make it. Or crash and burn...oh, God.

When she stepped onto the top floor, she was the last person aboard the elevator and entirely sure she should never be a motivational speaker.

The seventieth floor was as white and bright as the lobby below, but primarily empty. A receptionist tapped away on a keyboard. Across from her desk was a bright red couch for visitors, and three heavy oak doors against the far wall. Holly quietly walked up to the receptionist, her ID card clutched in her hand. The woman was a statuesque brunette wearing a chic sweater dress and a pair of fifties-inspired glasses. She stopped typing and looked up at Holly from behind her vintage eyewear.

"H-hi, I'm Holly McIntyre, the new assistant." She cleared her throat and held up her ID for proof, hoping the receptionist wouldn't notice the wild shaking of her hand.

"Lovely." The receptionist purred in a way that made Holly think of a cat that'd just spotted a defenseless mouse. "Go on in to Mr. Cantrell's office. Begin filing the papers on top of the filing cabinet in alphabetical order. He'll be in shortly to give you further instruction."

Holly waited to be dismissed, but took the woman's return to typing as her release. She walked back to the far wall to the three doors. One was labeled *'Meeting Room 1'*, the second *'Meeting Room 2'*, and the third read *'Cantrell'* in bold golden letters next to the door. Slowly, she grasped the handle and pushed the door open to let herself inside.

The room was large and richly furnished with a wall of floor-to-ceiling windows behind a stately desk. It was almost sterile-looking with no personal items to be seen between the imposing grandfather clock and leather armchairs. Holly looked around for a picture of her future boss, but the only art on the wall was a modern painting a man might've chosen—bright squares of red, blue, and black thrown onto a canvas. She thought a child could've put it together. It was nothing like the fine Italian frescos she'd seen online, nor like the famous reproductions of Monet paintings her parents had hanging in their restaurant back home. But what did she know about modern art? Holly had no doubt, however, that the simple piece had cost him thousands.

She placed her secondhand purse on one of the two guest chairs facing the desk and made her way to a very tall, large filing cabinet tucked into the corner of the room. Her hands began to sweat as she saw how monumental the cabinet was. While she was around five feet tall, the cabinet must have been seven feet high. Wondering if she could actually do her duties with this monstrous piece of office furniture, she tried reaching the stack of papers and manila envelopes, but her hands barely grazed the top of the cabinet. She glanced around for a stepladder, or a stool, but only saw the expensive chairs meant for guests. Not finding any other option, she pulled the empty chair toward the cabinet and hopped on, balancing on the plush cushion.

She had just grabbed the heavy stack when the office door burst open, causing her arms to fly up in surprise and the papers to scatter all over the floor, mimicking the worst kind of snowstorm. Holly immediately jumped off the chair with her hand covering her mouth to stifle a small shriek of surprise that escaped as a pained squeak. She had not been in the office more than five minutes and she'd already made a mess. What made it worse was that the only person to witness her shame was her boss, Jackson Cantrell.

***

Jackson raised a brow as he inspected his new assistant. She seemed as flighty as a bird, and almost as delicate.

"Oh, goodness! I'm so sorry, Mr. Cantrell...sir...I can't believe I..." Holly dropped back to the floor and began sweeping the papers into a pile with her quivering hands. "I'm sorry...I didn't...I couldn't reach..."

Jackson bent down to her level and began sorting the papers into small piles, slightly uncomfortable with the anxious woman fidgeting on his office floor. "I take it *you* must be my new assistant?"

"Y-yes. I'm Holly McIntyre." She looked up at him, green eyes glassy with fear. "I promise, I'm not always so clumsy."

He was taken aback upon seeing her fully. She was a pleasant-looking woman with a heart shaped face and full lips. As she lifted her emerald eyes to his, peeking at him from beneath her thick lashes, Jackson had to clear his throat. "Good to meet you, Holly."

"I'm really not like this. I'm very well organized and—"

Jackson held up a hand. "Please, it's really not a big deal. Why don't you just go get settled at your desk for now, and I'll fix this."

"My desk?" Her face was still pink from embarrassment, a feature Jackson found oddly endearing.

"Yes. Your office connects with mine so that I'll be able to reach you easily during business hours." He scooped the rest of the files up and stood, holding a hand out to her.

Holly smiled uneasily, showing off a row of perfectly white teeth. Her hand was delicate in his, and when she rose to standing, he was surprised to see she had rather shapely legs beneath the unflattering sack she wore. "Of course, Mr. Cantrell. Is there anything I can get for you? Latte? Coffee? Tea?"

He shot her a small smile, amused by her nervousness. "No, thank you. Go get settled."

Holly snatched her purse and tucked it under her arm, disappearing into her adjacent office. Jackson watched her leave, noting how that dowdy suit, and ugly shoes, did little to show her apparent charms. His other assistants were always well-groomed and expertly dressed, looking at ease in their designer clothes. Holly McIntyre almost seemed like a little girl playing dress-up in her mother's closet. He thought she would do better if she embraced her girl-next-door beauty instead of hiding it.

As he arranged the last of the files on his desk, he wondered if Holly had what it took to survive life in the big city.

***

Holly quickly grabbed her purse and went into the small room attached to Mr. Cantrell's office. It had the same large floor-to-ceiling window behind a modern white desk and red swivel chair that matched the theme in the lobby. On the desk were her new tools: a phone and a sleek computer, along with a notepad and a few pens. She decided she'd bring in a few things to make it more homey once she got settled. Perhaps a picture of her family and an orchid to brighten the room.

Holly sat behind her desk, taking deep breathes to calm her vivid embarrassment. She was thankful she had a boss who didn't seem to mind her sudden clumsiness. She felt so humiliated due to the fact that her ineptitude had been abundantly clear within ten seconds of meeting him.

She also couldn't believe how attractive he was. As soon as he stepped into the office she felt her face burn up. He wasn't old, balding, or fitted with a monocle and a cigar like the Monopoly Man. Instead he was a tanned, black-haired, blue-eyed, broad-shouldered god with a smile that only came with the perfect mix of breeding and confidence. He'd broken all the stereotypes Holly originally held. She briefly wondered how she'd manage to work for this man without swooning every time she brought him a latte.

After inspecting the drawers for further supplies, she bumped the computer mouse and the screen came to life, revealing a calendar. As she skimmed the dates, she noticed it was already filled for the next few weeks with Mr. Cantrell's meetings and business dinners. He obviously hadn't become so successful without constantly making deals and shaking hands. A few days during the next week were set aside for a visit from his mother, but that was the only glance into his personal life. It seemed he had no time for himself.

When the phone on her desk rang for the first time, Holly nearly jumped out of her seat. She fumbled with the headset before pushing a button labeled *answer* on the keypad. "G-good morning…Mister…um…" Her heart leaped into her throat as she instantly forgot her boss's name. *Cancella? Cochella? Cortell?*

"Who are you?" asked a woman with a heavy accent. Holly guessed she was Russian or Ukrainian, but she couldn't be sure. "Put Jackson on the phone."

Holly found a notebook in the top desk drawer and grabbed a pen while she worked to compose herself. "This is his assistant. Who might I say is calling?"

"He knows who I am. Put him on."

She bit her lip, unsure of what to do. "I'm going to need your name, ma'am."

The woman on the other end of the phone began yelling at her in Russian. Although Holly didn't know a single word, she was sure it wasn't exactly nice. "P-p-please hold." She pressed *hold* and then a button labeled *Cantrell*, and Jackson answered.

"Yes?"

"There's a very angry Russian woman on the phone demanding to speak with you, but she won't give me her name. Should I put her through?"

He sighed. "No. That's just Oxanna. Tell her I'm tied up in meetings."

Holly frowned before ending the call and putting Oxanna back on the line. "Ma'am? Mr. Cantrell is in meetings all day and cannot be reached. Can I take a message?"

"He is liar! I will come to office and he will talk! I will not be treated like this." Her words slipped back into Russian, and while Holly tried to take notes at first, she ended up nervously hanging up on the woman, guessing she was a little on the unstable side. She knew it was wildly rude of her, but her panic overcame all sense of politeness.

"Is she done?" Jackson's smooth voice startled her. He stood in the open door, casually leaning against the frame.

Holly took off her headset and tried to look like she wasn't flustered. "Yes, she's no longer on the line."

"Never let her calls through, or any other woman who wants to speak with me for personal matters. They will try to bully you into talking to me, but I'm hardly interested."

She made a little note saying *no women callers* and stuck it to the phone. "So, no personal calls during office hours at all?"

"I didn't say that. Just don't let any hysterical-sounding women through. This is my place of business, and if I wished to speak to them, they would have my personal number. The only person who might call to speak to me is my mother. She uses whatever number is most convenient for her at the moment."

"Okay, I'll make sure I patch her through."

"Also, if my campaign manager calls, make sure he's put through immediately, even if I'm in a meeting."

"Campaign manager?"

Jackson inspected one of his cufflinks, adjusting it before turning his attention back to her. "Yes. I'm running for mayor this year and voting season is quickly approaching."

Business tycoon, handsome bachelor, *and* future mayor? Holly couldn't believe he had enough hours in the day. His schedule certainly wouldn't make one think so. Surely he had time to sleep? Holly's mind drifted to a luxurious view of him in bed, but she hurriedly dispelled the thought. "I'll make sure he gets through. Can I do anything else for you?"

"No, you're doing a fine job." He nodded and stepped into his own office, leaving Holly alone.

The rest of the day passed uneventfully. She sorted files, took a few meaningless messages for her new boss, and didn't even make one coffee run. She had expected to be running around the city delivering paperwork and doing all the menial tasks a man like her boss would be too busy to take care of, but she found herself browsing the Internet more often than not. By the time she left for home, Mr. Cantrell had already gone for a dinner meeting and Holly locked up her office door behind her with a new set of keys that led to the floor's private bathroom, her office, and Mr. Cantrell's office. Being a New York City career girl was hardly the challenge she expected.

Chapter Two

Jackson leaned back in his office chair and tapped his fingers against the desktop. The raspy voice of his campaign manager, Denny Crew, assaulted his ear through the phone, and he turned down the volume slightly to make the unbearable conversation a little more comfortable.

"You're never going to get the Republican ticket," Denny said confidently. "No one wants to see a billionaire playboy take office."

"So, because I have money I should drop out?"

"It's not the money, it's the endless parade of models and b-list actresses you're all over the tabloids with. The Democratic ticket is pretty much settled with that lady who owns all the charter schools, so if you want to be the Republican nominee, you've gotta look like a Republican."

Jackson ran his hands through his hair. "I need to cheat on my non-existent wife and get caught with coke in my car?"

"This is no laughing matter. You only have a few more weeks to wine and dine some backers. But, as things are, you're not looking too hot."

"You're my campaign manager, so tell me what I have to do." He knew Denny was the best in the game, but he wondered if he was worth the scratch, considering Jackson felt he needed to pull every bit of help from his cold, dead fingers.

Denny heaved a long sigh into the phone. "You know what voters want to see? A candidate who's good with business and has strong family values. You gotta have a pretty wife, two-point-five kids, and a Labrador named Rocky. You got the business sense, but other than that you got squat."

"What the hell am I paying you for? Look, I don't have a wife and kids. Are you telling me to drop out of the race?"

"I'm telling you to look like a family man. If you wanna win, then get yourself a family," Denny said in an even voice. "A nice *normal* family."

Jackson chuckled dryly. He made it sound so easy. "Get myself a family? Just go down to the store and pick up a wife and kids?"

"Hey, I'm *not* going to tell you to deceive the mass public by entering into a sham relationship in order to snag the Republican ticket. But I *will* tell you that you finding a nice lady to get into a stable relationship with would certainly heighten your chances. So, if you got some farmer's daughter holed up in that office of yours, now is the time to wife her up."

"I'm not getting married to win."

"I'm not even telling you to get married for real, just to drop all those models and look like you're the stable family man we all know you're not."

Holly knocked on the doorframe, holding a folder against her chest. "Excuse me, sir, Holland is on line two. I brought you the corresponding files."

"Denny, I'm going to have to call you back." Jackson placed the phone back into the cradle, his gaze fixed upon Holly. Thoughts darted through his mind. He needed a wife, a family—a stable life to present to the voters. She needed to be attractive, quiet, pliable, and believable.

Holly stood there awkwardly, biting her bottom lip in that vaguely attractive way. She had only worked for him for a week, but he'd grown to see her as a fine employee and a trustworthy person. Having a non-disclosure agreement in her contract had certainly helped. Holly was new in the city, without any friends or relatives nearby. No one knew she worked for him, and she seemed attractive enough to fake being his arm candy for a few months. But as he took in her boxy dress and pinned-up hair, he wondered if he had any other options.

"Sir?" Holly looked around uncomfortably. "Is something wrong? Do you want me to tell Holland you'll call them back?"

Jackson picked up the phone, pressed two, and said, "My offer is twenty-two percent initial starting price with a seventy-three percent increase after five years. Talk it over and call me back." Once the receiver was back in the cradle, he turned to Holly.

"So, you don't need this anymore?" she asked, holding up the file.

"Holly," he began, buying time to collect his thoughts. "I recently read that you're from

Michigan."

"Recently? I thought you knew that when you hired me."

He chuckled, wracking his brain for other female options. "No, I had my old assistant select her replacement."

"You did?" A worried look grazed her features.

"Beth moved down to the eighth floor to work in accounting," Jackson explained, speculating about what Holly looked like without the librarian bun. "She was going to college while working for me, and as soon as she had her degree, I helped her obtain a position in her field. I'm not so cruel as to make someone select her replacement after firing her."

Holly reddened. "I didn't mean...I would never..."

"Please, Holly." He smiled, rather liking the way her cheeks flushed. She could do with a bit of a makeover, but the canvas was primed for paint. "You really do need to relax. I'm not a difficult man to work for, nor am I so involved in business that I'm incapable of a sense of humor. So, tell me about Michigan."

She shrugged slightly, looking down at her feet. But, he could see a small smile on her lips as she thought of home. "There's not much to tell, really. My parents own a little restaurant on Mackinac Island. It's a really small island off the coast of Michigan that you can only get to by boat and you can't even drive cars there. The roads are just for horses and golf carts. There are some historic buildings like an old fort, and whatever, so there're a lot of tourists in the summer."

"It's quiet the rest of the year?"

"Pretty much. There are still visitors, but nothing like in the summer."

"Must be nice to have a quiet winter." He made a mental note to find her a respectable hobby— horseback riding, reading to children at the library, maybe even hosting luncheons to raise money for cancer centers.

"I guess. But I was tired of the quiet winters and living in Michigan. That's why I came here."

"Well, hopefully it lives up to your expectations."

"It already has. I haven't really had the chance to do much sightseeing, but I'm hoping to visit a few museums or something this weekend." She grinned, her shyness ebbing with each passing moment.

"New York City does have a lot to offer." He glanced down at his Rolex. "I have a meeting in fifteen minutes. Email my mother for me, when you get a chance, and let her know travel plans haven't changed."

Holly nodded, back to business mode. "Anything else?"

"No, that's all for now. Thank you, Holly." Jackson knitted his brow, taking her in with pursed lips. He knew he needed to do it now or he wouldn't do it at all. "Holly, do you know anything about politics?"

She appeared perplexed for a moment. "Not much. I follow the presidential campaigns, but that's about it."

"When you see a candidate, what do you notice

about them?"

"Well, I guess what they stand for. Their families, the bills they support, that sort of thing."

"Exactly." Jackson snapped his finger. He hoped his enthusiasm would rub off on her. "You got it."

Holly frowned. "I'm sorry, what do I have?"

"A successful politician needs to be clear about his beliefs, have strong values that would translate well into laws, and a stable family. I am currently lacking one of those." Jackson stood up and walked over to the front of his desk. He leaned against the edge, arms crossed, peering into her green eyes. "Holly, when you began working here, your contract included a sturdy non-disclosure agreement, which is completely legally binding, so anything I say to you is strictly between us."

"I understand." Holly bit her lip again.

He stared at her mouth as he spoke, the gesture making it easier to imagine her as his fake fiancée. "Holly, if I'm going to win this race for mayor, I'm going to need a family."

"But you have a mother, right?"

"Voters don't care about that, especially with my mother's...um, reputation. They want to see a candidate with a spouse, some kids, and a white picket fence. They don't want to see a confirmed bachelor."

"I'm sorry, sir, I really don't understand where you're going with this."

"Holly, I need a wife, and I need one fast." He felt his usually calm demeanor crack as he firmly blurred the line between business and personal. "I need you to pretend to be my girlfriend...or fiancée."

Her eyes widened. "Excuse me?"

Jackson ran his hands through his hair again. "I know this sounds crazy, but I don't have a shot in hell at winning the Republican ticket, let alone the race, without some sort of family life. This isn't something I can do as a single man."

"Let me get this straight. You need me to pretend to be dating you?" Holly asked nervously, her cheeks paling. "I wouldn't be your assistant?"

Jackson shook his head. "No, you would be my girlfriend…wait, no, my *fiancée*, for a few weeks or so while my mother visits and until the elections are over. I would pay you your usual wages, of course, as well as overtime for any events or weekend activities you may have to accompany me on. You would also get a generous allowance for any clothes, transportation, or dining expenses you incur during your…job."

Holly lowered her brows into a suspicious glare and dropped the file she'd been carrying on his desktop. "I'm not a prostitute, Mr. Cantrell. This isn't *Pretty Woman*."

Jackson held up his hands defensively. He'd never seen her more than pleasant and placid, but the anger wafting off her small body heated the room. "I never said you were. I only need you to *look* like you're my fiancée. Come to dinner with us, take my mother out to lunch, pretend her boring stories amuse you. You'll have to go to a few campaign rallies and events, as well. It really might be more work than being my actual assistant," he added with a wry laugh that did little to calm the rays of apprehensive anger that made him sweat.

"But why do you need someone to pretend to be your fiancée? Can't you just get some Victoria's Secret model to go yachting with you?" Holly asked, planting her fists on her hips.

Jackson began to see a new side of Holly. Gone was the shy girl, replaced by a fiery woman. He would be lying if he said her newfound voice wasn't more than a little attractive. "Denny, my campaign manager, wants me to have a fiancée who isn't already in the tabloids and looks like a wholesome all-American girl."

"And I fit the bill?"

He nodded. "Yes, you do. I think you could even fool my mother."

"Your mother? Why would we have to lie to her?"

"She's very old-fashioned. She won't appreciate me pretending anything."

"Still, certainly you can just hire someone? There has to be someone believable."

"No one, especially my mother, would believe I was really settling down with some underwear model or aspiring actress. Mother imagines me with some Harvard graduate from old money who likes polo and vacationing in the Hamptons, or in the south of France. Someone cultured, poised, comfortable with the ridiculous demands of being a woman of leisure."

"But, I'm none of those things," Holly protested. "I didn't even go to college, let alone the south of France. The closest I've ever come to that is Canada."

Jackson smirked. "My mother doesn't know that."

"Why not just tell her?"

"She isn't known for her ability to keep a secret, especially one as juicy as this. It's safer if we have her fooled during the visit, as well."

She sat down in one of the armchairs and gaped. "I don't know if I feel comfortable helping you lie to your mom, let alone the whole city."

"My mother isn't a big fan of me entering into the realm of politics because she's afraid of it taking my focus away from the company. It's childish, but I want to prove to her that I can do this, that I can get something for myself. If she knew we weren't really a couple, she'd call me out in an instant."

"But won't I be in the papers or something?"

"Probably," he admitted. "But, most of the focus will be on me and my campaign. Since you're not already in the public eye, you should be slightly more protected from the paparazzi."

"If someone finds out, would we get in trouble? This sounds very illegal."

"It's not," he told her confidently. "Politicians lie all the time. They hide their mistresses and drug habits, make the voters think they're going to fix the education system and give free healthcare to all. This lie is no different than any of the others. In fact, it might be more innocent."

"What about when this whole thing comes to an end?"

Jackson paused. While finding a wholesome fiancée was almost in the bag, he hadn't thought ahead. Would they have a public breakup? Wait a few months after the election? How far was far enough to take the ruse? "Honestly, I haven't thought any further than the election. I'll give you a nice severance package and help you get any position in the city that you want. We'll cite an amicable breakup and go our separate ways for some reason or another."

"Won't the public hate me? I mean, you seem like a popular guy in the magazines."

He laughed, thinking back on how one magazine had called him a disgusting man whore. "Hardly. In fact, dumping me would probably make you more likeable. They'd think you were pretty smart for ditching me."

"This sounds so crazy," she whispered.

He knelt down next to the chair and softened his voice. "Holly, I *need* you." Jackson pleaded with her as he took her hands in his, then suppressed a laugh as he thought of how much this would seem like a proposal to anyone on the outside. In fact, it almost was one. "You're perfect for this job and I know I can trust you to see this through until after the election."

"I've only worked here, like, a week, and you're asking me to fake date you so you can become Mayor of New York. You know how ridiculous this sounds, right?"

"Holly, you're *perfect*," he said, squeezing her fingers. He worried he was laying it on too thick, but he had nothing else to lose. "You're pretty in that girl-next-door way, you're great at taking direction, and there's already a non-disclosure agreement in place so you could never out me to anyone. Please. I'm really in a tight spot right now and I'm not used to begging."

Peering down at him over her pointed nose, she heaved a sigh. "So, all I would have to do is basically hang out with your mom and go to dinner and fancy parties? This sounds like a lot of pressure. What's in it for me?"

He was taken aback by her sudden show of bravery. "Like I said, I would be paying you just like you were doing your regular job. You wouldn't be fetching coffee or answering phones. I would give you access to shopping and salon visits, that sort of thing. All you would need to do is pretend to be my fiancée from this point forward and not tell a soul that you were my assistant at any time, no matter what. "

"Salon visits?" Holly pulled her hand from his grasp and touched her honey blonde mane self-consciously. "Is something wrong with my hair?"

Jackson grimaced. Just like him to ask a woman for a favor and immediately insult her. "No, no, no. Not what I meant at all."

She glared at him. "Then what exactly did you mean?"

"I just meant…well, I…"

Holly giggled. It was a light, tinkling sound that immediately melted the tension. "I'm just messing with you, Mr. Cantrell. If you need me to get some new outfits to impress your mom and the voters, then I'll do it. But I have some conditions."

Jackson grinned, pleased that his absurd plan was falling into place. "Do tell."

She held up her fingers as she spoke, counting

out her terms. "I want us to stay professional when we're not in front of your mom, and all that. In public we're the picture of devotion, but otherwise we keep things professional. Like I said before, this isn't *Pretty Woman* and I don't want you telling all your buddies that I'm for hire. Secondly, I want your promise that you'll pull through when this is over, and help me get a good job in the city. I have rent and bills. On that note, you're paying me overtime when the clock hits six. Also, since you think I need a serious makeover, I'm telling you that I'm staying a blonde."

He nodded. "I've always preferred blondes, anyway."

"So we have a deal?"

"You've got yourself a deal, Holly," he said, holding out his hand for a shake.

"And you've got yourself a fiancée."

***

An hour later, Holly was strolling down 5th avenue with Jackson leading the way. As soon as she agreed to be his fake fiancée, he insisted on cancelling all of his meetings for the day and taking her shopping for a whole new wardrobe befitting someone of her apparent stature. Holly was not entirely comfortable with the idea of her boss buying her things, but it was technically her job to look like high society arm candy, so she was just going to enjoy it while it lasted.

The first store they went into was a typical New York City shop. The clothes were perfectly folded and aligned on pristine shelves. Slim, faceless, mannequins showed off form fitting dresses and held large alligator skin handbags in their plastic arms. In her shapeless beige business dress and sensible shoes, Holly felt totally out of place. She crossed her arms over her chest, hoping it hid her from view.

The saleswoman did not make her feel any better with her perfectly coiffed bun and sky-high legs clad in snakeskin boots. Her dark skin and almond eyes made her look exotic in a way Holly never could, thanks to her Scottish and Irish heritage.

"Mr. Cantrell, welcome back," the saleswoman greeted them warmly. "What can I help you with today?"

Jackson smiled and pushed Holly forward. "Alice, this is Holly, and we just wanted to go through a few selections and get her up-to-date with the latest styles."

Alice smiled. "Charmed," she purred, snapping her fingers to get the attention of a young, female sales associate, who stepped forward with a tray of glasses filled with freshly poured champagne.

Jackson gently picked up both glasses by the stems and passed one to a stunned Holly. She thought people only shopped like this in the movies, and her mind wandered back to *Pretty Woman* and she wondered if she was about to be kicked out in a dramatic fashion.

"Thanks," she whispered before taking a tentative sip.

"Well, Holly," Alice began. "How about you go wait in the dressing room and make yourself comfortable? I'll pick out a few things and we can go have a little fashion show."

Holly nodded wordlessly, and entered a brightly lit, mirror-filled room. The lights and multiple angles really gave Holly a chance to see herself. Now it was understandable why her boss wanted her to get new clothes. She was perfectly unappealing in her boxy dress. In this store with all of it's pretty, stylish things, Holly felt positively frumpy. She never really had a reason to wear nice things before. She spent her summers out on the lake in bathing suits and sundresses, her winters bundled up from the Michigan snow, and she never even went to prom. She finished her glass of champagne, willing it to hit her brain and loosen her up.

As she studied herself in the mirrors, she suddenly doubted she'd be able to pull off this scheme. She wasn't used to wearing heels and drinking champagne. The shoes hurt and the alcohol clouded her mind and made her dizzy. While she always had more than enough growing up in Michigan, she certainly wasn't particularly used to the finer things in life. If she looked as awkward as she felt, then Jackson's mother would be able to see right through her in an instant, when she arrived.

When Alice came into the room, she hung up two armfuls of clothes in a standing rack. "These look like your size, but I'll just run out and grab whatever you need if they don't fit." The woman took Holly's glass, motioning for her to inspect her selections.

"Thank you." Holly flipped through the full

hangers while she waited for Alice to leave. She looked at the saleswoman expectantly but it soon became abundantly clear that she wasn't going anywhere. Holly began to panic. Stripping down to her unmentionables in front of a stranger was terrible enough, but Alice was built like a glorious Amazon woman and had the confidence to match.

"Girl, please." Alice rolled her eyes, her poised demeanor gone to a more casual one. "Unless you're hiding a third arm under that sack, you have nothing I haven't seen before."

Holly quickly ditched her ill-fitting dress, trying to ignore the embarrassing heat creeping up her neck. Alice stood in the corner, holding out a black cocktail dress with a flourish, not making any effort to avert her gaze. When she saw Holly's equally frumpy beige bra and underwear combo, her jaw dropped.

"Darling, if you want to pull off an expensive look, you need to start with the bottom layer," Alice told her with a sigh, placing the dress back on the rack. "I can't put you in anything when you're wearing those hideous underthings."

Holly crossed her arms over her chest. "It's just underwear. No one is ever going to see it."

Alice huffed. "Look, I can make you transform from a frumpy little caterpillar into society butterfly if you let me."

"Do you really think I need new underwear?" Holly asked, daring another glance at her full-coverage panties.

"I think I know what I'm talking about. Just stay there and I'll grab you a few things," she answered, already leaving the room.

Holly wondered why Alice put such an emphasis on her underwear. It was not as if she'd be parading around in front of Jackson's mother in her bra and panties. But maybe she was just showing how unrefined she was by having unattractive underthings. *Maybe*, Holly thought, *she was only pretty in Michigan.*

To distract herself, she flipped through the rest of the hangers, taking in the blush skirts, cream blouses, and tailored jackets. But when her eye caught one of the price tags, she took a peek. She saw the number eight and then a zero...and then another. One short dress was eight hundred dollars! She could have fainted. Her entire wardrobe probably didn't cost as much as a simple top in that shop. Holly felt even cheaper than before.

Alice came back into the room with a handful of lace and silk that made Holly blush. "Here, put these on and don't be shy. We're both girls." She passed a blood red push-up bra and matching underwear into her hands.

Holly held up the tiny strip of lace and sighed. *Oh, the things I do for work.*

***

Jackson sat on a stiff couch outside the dressing room and waited for Holly's big reveal. Alice had come in and out of the dressing room several times, often carrying little pieces of frills and lace that he could only imagine did not cover all that much. But, this was Alice's area of expertise and he was sure

27

she could put Holly in just the right outfits to pass for a full-on society girl. He briefly felt a pang of guilt at the thought of placing his sweet assistant in this position. He still wasn't sure if the papers wouldn't pick her apart in an instant and find out who she really was. While he should have been more concerned about the press, Jackson was more worried about what his mother would think. The magazines likened her to a viper, and he tended to agree.

But it was possible that the idea of a daughter-in-law would soften her up in public, and private. She wasn't keen on him straying from the business world into the political arena. But Jackson was growing weary of constantly being in the office, cutting up companies, and laying off thousands. Things for Cantrell International were done for the money, but the things he could do as mayor would be for the people.

He was quite lucky that Holly was so compliant and didn't judge him too terribly about having to employ her in that manner. Sure he could have called one of his flings, but they were so fake and vapid there was really no way he could even begin to pretend to be interested in them for more than a fleeting night. Besides, most of the girls he went out with had pasts full of torrid love affairs and nude spreads in magazines. Holly's background was full of small town niceties and absolute normalcy that was borderline dull. Besides, he assumed she could hold a decent conversation about something other than what celebrities they might see at dinner or which shoes went with what dress. Holly had substance, and although she was worried, Jackson felt she could fit in with his crowd nicely.

Alice popped her head out of the dressing room door. "Mr. Cantrell, are you ready to see a bit of what I've selected for her?"

Jackson sat up in the seat and nodded, fully ready to bring the job to an end. "Of course." He had waited nearly an hour, after all. And although he was the one who'd dragged Holly on this shopping trip, he really despised being stuck waiting on the 'boyfriend couch.'

Holly slowly stepped out from behind Alice and to the small strip of tile in front of where Jackson sat. Her cheeks were pink and she kept her gaze focused on the ground as she awaited his inspection. Jackson's eyes widened in surprise as he saw what Alice had placed her in. A pale pink, knee-length dress hugged her bust and flared out at the waist, demurely showing off a figure that would really turn heads. He had no idea that under all the baggy clothes Holly wore, she was hiding an ample chest, a tiny waist, and a pair of shapely legs that ended in cream high heels that were a far cry from her usual clunky shoes.

"Is it all right?" she asked quietly.

"Y-yes. It's fine. Everything's fine. We'll take it all." He dug his wallet out of his suit pocket and extended his Black Card to Alice, his hand shaking slightly.

Alice took the credit card and looked at Jackson curiously. "Don't you want to see what else she has? I've found quite a bit that fit her so it's basically a full wardrobe."

"No," Jackson croaked, finally looking away from Holly. "I trust you. Package it all up and have it delivered to her apartment. And she's wearing this dress out."

He could hardly bring himself to do more than glance at Holly. She filled out the clothes to perfection and her honey colored hair was down, falling down her back in gentle waves that made him want to wrap it around his fist. The thought dissipated, but left his designer slacks more than a bit tight.

Holly looked up shyly from her new, expensive shoes to Jackson when she noticed him staring. "That was faster than I thought. But, I figured you would want to see everything before you bought it."

"It's not necessary. This is one of the top stores in the city. Anything that Alice brought in for you will be more than satisfactory. She's also very discreet and would be more than happy to assist you in the future," he told her as Alice came back to deliver his card and get Holly's home address. "Besides, nothing on you could look bad, so I don't think we have any reason to worry."

As Holly wrote down her home address, Jackson could see by the look Alice gave the notepad that she recognized that Holly wasn't living in a very rich neighborhood, but had the courtesy not to say anything. Jackson slipped his wallet back into his jacket pocket, then steered Holly gently outside and onto the street.

"So, they'll just take all this stuff to my apartment?"

"Of course. Are you interested in getting a bite to

eat?" Jackson asked as they made their way toward a line of restaurants. He wasn't particularly hungry, but the thought of having Holly on his arm in public was strangely appealing.

"Sure," Holly replied, fidgeting a bit in her dress. "As long as you don't have anywhere you need to be."

"Not a place in the world. I cancelled all of my appointments so we can get you primped, remember? I figure that if you can fool my mother, then I'm pretty sure you'll fool all of New York. Besides, I think we should get to know each other a little better so you can stop looking so awkward around me." He shot Holly a bright smile and grinned wider as she began to blush. Jackson liked that he had some effect on her. She was making him feel a bit lighter, too. "See? You get red whenever I talk to you. We need to get more comfortable interacting."

"I'm Irish," Holly said indignantly. "I redden easily."

"Whatever you say," he replied, holding the door open for her at the first restaurant they passed. Jackson couldn't help but snag a quick look at her ass as she passed him, noting how the fabric of her skirt hid the area from view. It was a disappointment. "I would still like to get to know you."

The hostess led them to Jackson's usual table. It was slightly secluded with a fine view of the busy street. Once they were seated and had ordered their food, Jackson decided it was high time to talk. He swirled the scotch in his glass and studied her over the rim.

"What?" She pinked, averting her eyes from his gaze.

"Tell me about yourself. I think it's appropriate that I know my fiancée at least a little bit," he prompted, folding his long-fingered hands upon the table next to his drink.

Holly shrugged. "There's not a whole lot to know, and a lot of it you've probably already read in my employee file."

"All I really know is where you grew up. Do you have any siblings?" he asked, urging her to continue.

"I have a younger sister who's a total brain. She starts at Michigan State University next semester."

"Tell me more. Favorite foods, do you have any pets, anything?"

"I like all foods and my sister has this nasty cat who hates everything. I always wanted a dog, but since she's younger than me, she got her pick at the animal rescue place. I thought maybe I'd go and adopt one once I got settled in, but I would feel bad getting one when I keep such long hours."

"I always had dogs growing up," he said. "My parents traveled a lot so I guess they decided giving me animals to take care of would make me too busy to realize they were gone."

"So you were lonely as a kid?" Her eyes softened and Jackson felt a strange pang akin to embarrassment. He had meant his statement to be a joke, not a confession of childhood abandonment.

"I guess, but I have a hard time rationalizing complaining about being lonely when I had a lot of opportunities that other people didn't. If my parents didn't leave me to raise myself, then I probably wouldn't be how I am today."

"Successful?"

"Among other things," he said vaguely, taking a sip of his drink. "I read that you never worked as a personal assistant before. Why move here to do something you could do anywhere?"

"It's not like I've always dreamed of being a personal assistant. I actually want to eventually be an event planner," Holly admitted, her cheeks flushing.

"An event planner? Why?"

Holly seemed to relax more, the tension in her shoulders easing as she spoke about her passion. "I've done a lot of things back home with the catering business my parents run out of their restaurant. Nothing big, just small weddings and baptism parties."

"And you enjoy it?"

She nodded earnestly. "Very much so. There's nothing like making someone's day special and making them happy. I know it would be a ton of work to even begin to do a large scale event like they have in New York, but I'd be up for the challenge."

"I suppose that was a very brave move for you. You seem to have a good head on your shoulders. So, I have to ask, how does this whole thing seem to you? Honestly."

"Having lunch with my boss?"

"No, pretending to be engaged to your boss. It must make me seem pretty pathetic." He studied her as she paused to think. The pale dress made her look more feminine and delicate, but her expressive green eyes flashed.

"I mean, sure, it's really weird to think about, but I guess that's what a good personal assistant would do. I just don't understand why."

He sighed. "It's pretty complicated so just bear with me. When my father died a few years ago, it tore my mom up pretty badly and I was all she had left. She poured all of her efforts into making me have a family with a ton of kids so I wouldn't be completely alone if something happened to her."

"That's sweet of her, though, to worry like that."

"Not particularly. She hates everyone I've ever dated. Granted, I've only dated bland women who were more interested in my wallet than they were in me. With the elections coming up and all the press surrounding it, I can't have her come to see me and see that I'm alone. She would worry that I was spreading myself too thin. Besides, I'm tired of her constantly forcing me to have dinner with all of her friends' daughters. If she could arrange a marriage for me, I know that she would in a heartbeat."

"Do you really think having me around will help you win the election?"

"Bachelors don't win elections. People don't want to vote for someone they think isn't good with commitment."

"So, are you?"

"Am I what?"

"Bad at committing?"

He shrugged. Many women had asked him that over the years; they would roll over in bed, pouting

34

when he slipped from the sheets, making excuses about business meetings and work calls. "Maybe. I think I'm just too busy to settle down right now. I'm still working on my business and enjoy not having to answer to anyone."

"How much more does your business need to grow before you think about taking some time off?"

"It's not just my business. I have my hands in a whole bunch of ventures—hotel chains, publishing houses, charities, and now politics."

"Then I guess if you become mayor, you won't be able to ever stop working."

"I suppose not."

"Then why go for it? Isn't being a business tycoon enough?"

He pursed his lips. While women had always asked him about wedding rings, babies, and expensive vacations, no one had ever asked him that. "It should be, but it's not. I want to accomplish a lot during my life, and the way I see it, my life might end tomorrow. I wouldn't want to leave this world without doing things that were worth something. Politics is a gamble. People love you, hate you, trust you, want you gone, but you can always try to make their lives better no matter how they feel."

"And by being mayor, you think you'll be able to accomplish that?"

"Being mayor is just the start. I'd like to end up in Congress, or the Senate, if I can."

"So is this going to be a recurring job for me?"

Jackson laughed. "No, I think once I have a bit of experience in this department, it'll be enough for the public."

"Okay, then what about your mom? What happens when she realized there isn't really going to be a wedding and that I'm just your assistant?"

"I still didn't get that far." He smiled grimly. "I'm just taking this one step at a time and hoping for the best. You know, when I hired you to be my fiancée, I never even asked if you were seeing anyone."

"I'm not."

"No high school sweetheart waiting for you back in Michigan?" he teased, trying to lighten the mood and take the focus off himself.

Holly shook her head and smiled. "No. I had one of those, but he's old news. It's just you and me, sir."

"Jackson," he corrected as their waitress placed two impeccably designed dishes before them. He waited until she left before saying, "If we're supposed to be getting married, you need to call me by my first name. Pretend you like me."

"I do like you." The next words came out in a rush, "As a boss."

"Well, you need to act like you like me as a *fiancée*. Madly in love—can't live without me, love me like the day is long."

"Then maybe you should give me a raise first," she mumbled into her glass.

Jackson let loose a deep laugh. "You know, you're something else. I can tell this is going to work out just fine."

Chapter Three

When Holly arrived back at her apartment later that day, she saw a pile of pristine white boxes next to her front door. They were each wrapped up with a red ribbon and had her name written on them in elegant script. She was surprised no one had stolen them, but her only neighbor was a girl who lived in the apartment next to hers and Holly had yet to meet her, anyway.

She opened her front door and pushed the boxes inside before locking up behind her. She kicked off her new heels and went to work unwrapping the clothes. Opening all the boxes full of beautiful things made it feel a bit like Christmas in September. Although she hated to sound so greedy, she felt a rush as she unboxed each beautiful item. Each piece was gently covered in tissue paper and she briefly wondered how many trees died so that they could be made into boxes for her fancy new dresses.

She ended up with more than eight daytime dresses, four cocktail dresses, three skirts, two blouses, purses, some designer jeans, several tops, as well as numerous pairs of expensive high heels that Alice promised would not result in her breaking her neck. The masses of clothes could barely fit into her tiny closet.

Holly had just finished putting her new things away and changing into a t-shirt and a yoga pants when there was a quiet knock on her door. She peered through the peephole to see a woman with brown curly hair and freckled cheeks standing on the landing. Holly unlocked the door and poked her head out. "Hi, can I help you?"

"Yeah, are you Holly?"

She nodded. "Yes, is there something I can help you with?"

The woman held out a small package. "This was slipped into my mail slot by mistake. I'm Amber. I live next door."

Holly opened the door wider and took the box. It simply said *Holly-Jackson*. "Thanks so much. Do you want to come in?"

"Sure," she answered, glancing at her watch. "I have a little bit of time before my shift."

"What do you do?" Holly led her into the apartment and offered her a seat on the couch.

She indicated her plain blue scrubs. "I'm a nurse, so I keep weird hours. I guess that's why I haven't been able to meet you yet. What about you?"

"I work as a personal assistant," Holly answered, before remembering that she had promised Jackson about not telling anyone about her job.

"Coffee slave, right?" Amber giggled. "When I was in college, I tried doing that to pay for tuition, but I couldn't keep up with this lady's crazy demands. I was taking care of her and all three of her yappy dogs. How bad do you have it?"

"Well, I guess I *used* to be a personal assistant. Now I'm…an event planner." Holly hated to lie, but if she was going to pretend to have a job, then she would at least pick one she liked.

Amber looked around at all the boxes. "It looks like business is going well."

"Oh, these are all gifts."

Her neighbor raised a brow. "Gifts?"

Holly blushed, realizing what Amber must think of her explaining the piles of new things as *gifts*. While she might have guessed Holly was a sugar baby, she wasn't far off the mark. "They're from my boyfriend."

"Ugh, I wish I had your boyfriend," she said with a giggle.

"Yeah, Jackson's a great guy. I guess he thought I needed an update in my wardrobe."

"Well, he has great taste. Does he work in the city?"

"Yeah, at Cantrell international."

Amber held up a hand, her brows raised. "Wait. You're dating a guy named Jackson who works at Cantrell International? Don't tell me you're dating *the* Jackson Cantrell."

Holly bit her lip, hoping her neighbor didn't see through the lies. "Yeah, do you know him?"

"Do I *know* him? I wish! He's only been named one of the top bachelors in New York City for the past, like, five years."

"Oh, I didn't know that."

"Girl, you have to tell me…is he as delicious in person as he is in the magazines?"

Holly felt heat pool in her cheeks and she quickly attempted to cover it up with a shade of her hair. "Well, yeah, he is," she admitted, feeling open to the idea of having a New York City girlfriend to gossip with.

"You're so lucky! I can't believe I'm living next to the girlfriend of Jackson Cantrell. And you seem so normal."

"Thanks?"

"I didn't mean it in a bad way. I've just seen him with models and whatever, so it's nice to see that famous people are real people like us, you know? But enough about your man. I'm so glad you moved in. The last guy who lived here was a total mess. Never paid his rent, always took my magazines. You seem totally ordinary."

"I try to be."

"How long have you guys been together?"

"About a year," Holly lied, thinking that was a respectable timeframe.

Amber's brows rose. "Wow, I would have never guessed. You're not from the city, are you?"

Holly stifled a disappointed frown. She apparently still had that small-town smell. "Nope. I'm from Michigan. This is my first time to New York City."

Amber's eyes got wide. "So you're telling me that you've never even visited here and then just decided to live here?"

"It sounds crazy if you say it like that. I flew in for a few days for my job interview and to get an apartment, but otherwise, that's pretty much what happened."

"That's amazing. I love a good romance." She glanced down at her watch. "Well, I have to get to work. Let's go out for drink sometime."

"That would be fun. It would be nice to know someone here."

Amber grinned. "Well, Miss McIntyre, as your first official New York City friend, I'd like to say welcome to the Big Apple. Knock on my door anytime and we'll hang out."

Once she had locked up behind Amber, Holly focused on the package Jackson had sent her. He must have had someone drop it off, as the only things written on the brown packaging was her name and his own. She gently ripped off the paper to find an iPhone with a note attached to the front of the box.

Holly,

Since you're now working as my fiancée, I'm going to need a way to keep in contact with you. This phone is a secure line so we can speak freely without any chance of interception. It's all set up and my home number, cell phone number, and office numbers are already plugged in.

—Jackson

Ps. You have a spa appointment at three tomorrow followed by dinner with my mother at seven. Wear something nice.

Holly popped the cellphone out of the box and watched the screen come to life. In one day, she got a fiancé, a new wardrobe, a top of the line cellphone to replace her old one, and a friend. Maybe living in New York City wasn't going to be so bad after all.

Chapter Four

At quarter to three the next day, Holly heard a firm rapping at her front door. When she looked out of the peephole, she saw an imposing man in a suit standing on her landing.

"Can I help you?" she asked through the door, suddenly thinking about all the murders her mother had told her about. At over six feet tall, and more than three hundred pounds of pure muscle, there would be nothing stopping him from snapping her in half like a twig. A pair of beefy hands were clasped in military fashion at his waist. The man's neck alone was thicker than one of Holly's thighs. For a moment, Holly considered making a mad dash for her phone.

"I am here to collect Miss Holly for her appointment. I'm Rick, Mr. Cantrell's driver." His voice, which was soft and meek sounding, was in stark contrast to his daunting figure.

Holly opened the door a crack, wide enough for Rick to pass her an embossed business card. He was indeed Jackson's driver and bodyguard. "Why did he send me a driver? I could have taken a taxi."

"Mr. Cantrell wants his fiancée to be expertly taken care of," Rick explained as he stepped aside to allow Holly to open the door and exit her apartment. "He has informed me of your arrangement and had entrusted me as your personal bodyguard and driver for the remainder of your agreement." He reached into his pocket and pulled out a sleek new credit card. "Mr. Cantrell also had this printed for your use. It has no limit and you can charge whatever you need."

She took the card that was engraved with her name. It was real, but the feelings of the hard plastic in her hand felt unnatural. "I can't accept this."

"It's already been arranged. It's part of your new salary."

"Wow, okay."

"Now, we really must be going or you'll be late."

Holly snapped back into focus. "Right, of course." She went to the kitchen and grabbed her purse and keys. As soon as the front door was locked behind her, Rick led the way down the stairs and opened the door onto the street after taking a quick peek around. He was thorough.

Holly blushed as she saw the sleek, black town car parked in front of her building and muttered a quiet thanks when Rick opened the back door for her. As soon as he was inside and they began their drive, she felt increasingly more awkward. She wasn't used to being driven around like royalty and she wasn't really sure why her boss would think she was in need of protection. "Um, Rick? Can I ask you something?"

"Anything, Miss Holly," he answered, never taking his eyes off the road.

"Why do I need a bodyguard?"

"Mr. Cantrell is a very important man. There are many people who would like to ruin his businesses. While you are in no danger, I am here as a precaution."

His words did nothing to ease her worries. "Then is Mr. Cantrell in danger?"

"He, too, has a guard to shadow him on business trips and various events. I am his usual guard, but he placed me with you until your arrangement comes to a close."

"So, you know about us being—"

"Not really in a relationship?" Rick offered. "I know everything."

"I guess he really trusts you."

"I have worked for Mr. Cantrell for a long time. He's a good boss and I'm happy to be in his employment."

"Did he tell you what he wants done with me today at the salon?"

"No, but I assume he has called ahead to arrange your treatments." He pulled over in front of a brightly lit salon that boasted a black and white sign displaying the name **'Cosmo's'**. Rick exited the car and opened the door for Holly before she even had her seatbelt off. Holly wondered if they were even allowed to park on the side of the road like this, but assumed her boss had some sort of special billionaire license plate or something. "I'll be waiting just outside. If you feel there is any danger, just raise your arm above your head or dial the number two on your phone. That's the speed dial to my cellphone."

"You really don't have to wait here for me. I would feel really bad knowing you were just sitting in here while I was getting my nails done or whatever."

"It's my job. Don't worry about me."

"Can't you just come in?"

"If that would make you feel safer, then I will."

"No, I mean, there must be some kind of massage for men or a pedicure."

Rick raised his bushy eyebrows. "You want me to actually *attend* a spa appointment?"

She shrugged. "Why not? I'm sure Mr. Cantrell won't mind. If this card is really for me to charge whatever I want, then I want you to come in and enjoy yourself. I really can't get pampered while you're sitting out here in the car."

"Whatever you want, Miss Holly," he said, resigning himself to his fate.

The salon was more than Holly could have imagined. The waiting room was comfortable with soft purple couches and elegant paintings of women with elaborate hairstyles. A stone fountain made up of two fat cherubs holding vases sat in the center of the room and poured water that complemented the gentle violin music. It was much different than the little discount shop Holly used to go to back in Michigan.

A spindly woman in black greeted them as soon as they entered. "Good afternoon. Holly, I presume?"

"Um, yes. Jackson Cantrell made this

appointment for me."

Her mouth split into a thin smile. "Of course. We have all been in a tizzy imagining the woman who has stolen the heart of Jackson Cantrell." The woman's voice was unnaturally high.

Holly reddened and she could have sworn she heard Rick cough to cover up a short chuckle. "I guess he already told you guys what I'm coming in for?"

"No, he merely asked us to set aside a few hours for whatever treatments you would like." She produced a heavy leather-bound book from behind the desk and handed it to her. "Take your time and select whatever you would like from our menu."

There were lists and lists of different facials, mud baths, steam massages—there was no way she would ever know what to choose. "I'm not really a spa person. Is there anything you would suggest?"

The woman looked her over carefully. "I would suggest a trip to the steam room, the lotus facial, manicure, pedicure, trim up the hair, shine treatment to bring back some light and brightness, eyebrow waxing...let's just make it a full body wax, perhaps a full body seaweed wrap?"

"No seaweed, and I am not a big fan of steam rooms either." Holly looked up at Rick. "I'm getting him a massage, too, or whatever else he wants."

"Of course." The woman nodded, bringing her hand up to her ear to press a button on her headset. "The Cantrell appointment is ready for her treatments and I'm sending in a gentleman for a deep tissue massage."

***

"Daaahling," Cosmo cooed, lifting up several strands of Holly's blonde hair. "Lovely color, but it is clear you and conditioner are not on speaking terms."

"I condition," Holly protested from her spot in Cosmo's salon chair. In the past two hours, she had been massaged, waxed, had a floral-smelling facial, and had her nails shaped perfectly and coated in pale pink polish. Now she was sitting with the salon master himself, waiting for him to work his magic.

"No, daaahling, do not lie to Cosmo. Cosmo knows all." The thin man danced around the chair, randomly tilting her head and whispering something to his assistant. "Cosmo will start with a deep conditioner followed by a shine serum. Your hair is so dead, Cosmo will have to bring in the Jaws of Life to save it!"

"Is it really that bad?" she asked, looking up at his perfectly tanned face.

He nodded, his Botoxed skin making a perfect mask. "Yes, but Cosmo will fix. Cosmo will turn this bird's nest into a golden cascade of light and glory." He picked up a bottle and squirted the green contents into his hand. "Now, let's begin."

***

"All finished, Miss Holly?" Rick asked as she exited the salon.

"Yes, did you like your massage?"

He smiled. "Very much so, thank you."

48

"Don't thank me, thank Mr. Cantrell." She giggled, sliding into the back seat. Once inside, she inspected herself in her compact mirror. The woman looking back at her was a far cry from the mousy blonde she'd been when she first arrived in the city. Her hair was thick and healthy, falling down past her shoulders in beautiful waves, while her skin had a natural glow. Cosmo had done her makeup in gentle, earthy tones that accented her features perfectly without taking away from them. He had even showed her a few tips and bagged up some pallets for her to take. Holly didn't look like a different person, exactly, just a polished version of her ideal self.

As soon as Rick dropped her off at her front door, it was time for her to get ready for dinner. Holly stared at her closet. There was a big difference between the girl from Michigan who lived in jeans and sweaters, and the girl who was going out to a fancy dinner in New York City dressed to the nines. Her new clothes were all structured silk dresses in garment bags and skirts covered in lace with high heels that gave her an extra few inches in height that she'd never had before. At first, she was worried about the job her boss had given her, but what could be so bad about getting paid to dress up and go out to dinner?

She smiled as she flipped through the hangers and selected a random garment bag to unzip. Holly picked a dark blue dress with a matching lace overlay that was form fitting, but came to the knee and covered up to her collarbone, making it conservative enough. The three-quarter sleeves also added to the beauty of the simple dress, which she topped off with a pair of muted gold pumps. When she saw herself in a full-length mirror, she was stunned with what she saw. The woman who looked back at her was absolutely perfect and would have been at home in high society. Now it was up to her to play the part.

***

Jackson sat alone at their table at the Plaza Hotel waiting for Holly and his mother to arrive. He tapped his fingers against the tablecloth, an impatient habit he was likely to never break. While his plan seemed perfect on the drive over, it now gave him uncharacteristic anxiety. His mother was a difficult woman to get along with, let alone please, and he wasn't sure if Holly was truly up to the task. Either way, it was too late to turn back.

As his gaze skimmed the dining room, he saw a woman enter. He blinked as a waiter led her closer. This woman was gorgeous—hourglass body, shiny blonde hair that framed a flawlessly made-up face, and sky-high legs clearly visible between the hem of a designer dress and a pair of Louboutin shoes.

"Holly?" he whispered, his voice oddly raspy. He stood to greet her, kissing her on the cheek. His lips lingered a moment longer than he intended. "Holly, you look fantastic."

"Thank you, sir...I mean, *Jackson*." She blushed prettily, looking down at the floor. "So, I fit the part?"

"Perfectly," he told her, pulling out her chair.

Holly sat down, placing her gold clutch in the table. "Where's your mother? Isn't she joining us?"

"Momentarily." Jackson glanced around the dining room, almost wishing his mother wasn't on her way. Holly was far more exquisite than he'd originally thought possible, and he found himself wishing he could have his fiancée all to himself. "She's usually late for things, but I needed to give you something, anyway."

"Give me what? I have a phone, a closet full of clothes, and overtime pay."

He reached into the breast pocket of his jacket and pulled out a ring. "It occurred to me today that, although you're dressed like my fiancée, you hardly look like one without a ring."

"Oh, my." Holly reached out and slipped the golden band onto her perfectly manicured finger. It featured a large oval diamond flanked by smaller, circular stones on either side.

"Does it fit the part?" he teased, content that she seemed so star-struck.

"It's so…big."

Jackson raised an eyebrow in amusement. "I give you an eighty-thousand dollar engagement ring and that's your reaction? You really are a strange woman, Holly."

Holly sputtered. "Eighty thousand dollars? Are you serious?"

"I make a good deal of money. I couldn't have my fiancée running around with a pitiful rock on her hand. It would make me look like quite the miser." It was true. When he'd called up his jeweler to prepare a sheet of selections, he thought the old

51

man would have a stroke. Even someone whose business it was to deal with diamonds couldn't contain his disbelief.

"But was it really necessary to buy an actual ring? You could have totally went to Canal Street and got a fake one for a few dollars."

He shook his head. "Mother would notice. That woman knows a thing or two about diamonds." He suddenly stood with a smile. "Speak of the devil."

"My boy," the woman said in a French accent.

Jackson stood, kissing his mother on both cheeks. "Mother."

He watched as Holly rose from her seat. The two women were polar opposites. While Holly was curvaceous and golden, his mother had the spindly body of a model with fashionably graying black hair and a steely gaze.

"You must be Holly."

Holly smiled and held out her hand. "It's so nice to meet you, Mrs. Cantrell."

She waved her hand in exasperation and took the seat Jackson offered her. "Please, call me Ursula. I cannot stand to feel old."

"You're hardly old, Mother," Jackson reminded her with a grin.

"Now that my son is getting married, I certainly feel that way." She called a waiter over and ordered a bottle of Cristal. "There are no celebrations without fine champagne. Now, Holly, tell me about you. To be honest, I never heard of you until a week ago."

Holly bit her lip as she sat. "What would you like to know?"

"Everything," Ursula insisted as the waiter returned with their champagne. "You were such a secret."

"Well I, um..." Holly glanced at Jackson, who immediately noticed her distress.

"There weren't any secrets, Mother," Jackson stated calmly, trying to diffuse the situation. "I merely waited to tell you about Holly until I was sure that our relationship would work."

"Good." Ursula took a sip of her drink, her red lips miraculously not leaving a mark on the spotless glass. "You know how I hate to have my time wasted. But, still, I would like to know about you, Holly. Did you go to school? Do you live in the city? What do your parents do?" She trained her eyes on Holly, waiting.

Holly looked over at Jackson, who gave her an encouraging nod. They hadn't gone over an exact script, but he was sure she could figure it out. In fact, having her pressed by his mother was the perfect test. If Holly could make it through Ursula's interrogation, she would be ready for the media. "My parents are in the restaurant business."

"Restaurateurs?" Ursula sounded impressed. "Family business, I assume?"

Holly nodded. "Yes, back home in Michigan."

"You're from Michigan?" Ursula raised a perfectly sculpted eyebrow.

Jackson saw Holly square her shoulders, taking on a more confident look. "Yes, but I've been in New York for a while now."

"And what do you do with yourself now that you're here?"

"Oh, this and that," Holly answered. Jackson saw her recently acquired strength dwindle.

"So, no career then?"

Holly's eyes widened. "Well, I wouldn't say that."

"Holly's an aspiring event planner," Jackson said, recalling one of their previous conversations. "She's very creative."

"Then you're certainly in the perfect city. Perhaps I'll set you up with one or two of my friends. They are always having parties and such." Ursula waved her hand again and motioned for Jackson to top off her glass.

Holly's mouth opened in surprise. "That would be amazing. Thank you so much."

"Of course. We are *famille* now," she told her with finality as the waiter came to take their orders.

Jackson squeezed Holly's hand under the table, surprising himself with the organic feel of the motion. "You're doing great," he whispered as his mother busied herself with ordering complicated dishes for the table.

"Now," Ursula said as the waiter hurried away. "Let me see it."

"See what?" Holly asked.

Ursula rolled her eyes. "The ring, silly girl."

"Oh, right." Holly lifted her hand for Ursula's inspection, her cheeks pink with embarrassment.

"It is gorgeous, my son." Ursula smiled warmly at Jackson. "Tell me, how did it happen?"

"Holly tells it so much better," Jackson deflected smoothly, curious how she would handle the question. "Don't you?"

Holly paled, but didn't miss a beat. "Well, one evening, we decided to go for a walk through the city. We came to Times Square and we stopped in the center, which was strangely empty. Suddenly, I heard music. It was an entire string band. Then, all of the electronic billboards went completely black." Holly paused and glanced at Jackson. She told a good story. "On the board, I saw a flash of pictures of Jackson and I out to dinner, dancing, at the park, on the beach…and at the end of the slideshow were the words, *Holly, will you marry me?* When I turned to look at him, he was on one knee with a ring box in his hand."

Ursula wiped away a stray tear with a red lacquered finger. "Oh, that is *très belle*, my son. Who knew you were such a romantic?"

"Certainly not me, Mother," Jackson answered, his face showing a faint trace of astonished amusement. "Certainly not me."

* * *

"Holly, you did fantastically," Jackson told her as he walked her to her door. "It was a rocky start, but after you told her that engagement story, you had her eating out of the palm of your hand! Where did you get that from?"

"I read it in a book." She blushed and turned her head, causing a stray strand of hair to slide over her cheek.

Jackson fought the urge to tuck the blonde lock behind her ear. "Well, it was perfect. I couldn't have asked for anything more."

"I'm glad I'm living up to my boss's expectations."

"And more," he said. Although they had been standing in front of her door for some time, neither made any move to part. "I mean it, Holly. I really appreciate what you're doing for me."

"Don't worry about it. What are personal assistants for?"

"And you'll be free to take my mother shopping tomorrow, right?"

"Shopping?"

"Yes. I think it's really all she does," he explained with some amusement. "The woman has a serious problem."

"I already have a ton of clothes now. But if that's what you need me to do, I can go."

He shook his head with a chuckle. "You are the only girl I've ever met who doesn't like shopping with my money."

"Oh, that's right. I forgot you gave me a credit card."

"You're the first girl who's ever said that, too." He laughed again, his words truer than he'd like to admit.

"I've never had one before. I feel a little weird using it."

"Rick's sure glad you decided to at the spa today. I'm pretty sure he's going to make me add weekly spa visits to his contract."

"Anything to boost company morale, sir." Holly grinned.

"Jackson, remember?"

"Right, sorry. It's going to take some getting

used to."

"Of course." He leaned down and brushed his lips against her cheek, a hasty gesture that he couldn't help but make. "Goodnight, Holly."

"Goodnight…Jackson."

Chapter Five

When Holly stepped out of the town car at Cantrell International, she was assaulted by a barrage of flashing bulbs. A swarm of reporters and photographers called out to her as Rick pushed them away to make a path. Confused, Holly gripped the back of his suit jacket and held on until the building's security came outside to order the horde from the front doors.

As soon as she was safely inside, Holly straightened her plum wrap dress and smoothed her hair into place, trying to blink away the white spots that danced in her line of vision. "What was that all about?" she asked Rick as he walked her past the usual security at the front desk and to the elevator. "Is there a celebrity here or something?" She glanced around, hoping to catch sight of Cher or Britney Spears.

"I'm not sure. Perhaps Mr. Cantrell will have a better idea. I'll stay here and wait for Ms. Ursula."

"Thank you," Holly muttered as the doors closed behind her. She checked her red lipstick in the mirrored walls and tried to steady her erratic breathing. The excitement of the crowd outside was palpable and she longed to find out who the celebrity was. Hopefully, Jackson was important enough to get her a meet and greet. Holly knew her mother would be shocked if she found out she'd met a real, live celebrity.

"Holly." Jackson was standing outside the elevator doors on his floor, obviously waiting for her. "Are you okay?"

"Fine, just confused," she replied, following him into the office. The receptionist gave her a tight, slightly angry look as she passed. Holly thought someone had a case of the sour grapes. "Do you know what those photographers wanted?"

"To see the future Mrs. Cantrell," he answered dryly.

He felt her knees go weak and her heart hammer against her breast. "Me? But we're not actually engaged," Holly hissed once they were behind the closed doors of his office.

"Apparently, we've done such a fine job of pretending at dinner last night that someone noticed and the press has gotten hold of the story."

"But why do they care?"

"Because I've been in magazines about being a bachelor and all that nonsense. To society and the tabloids, you're the secretive woman who's locked down the richest bachelor in New York City. You've managed the impossible."

Holly slumped down in one of the seats. "Are they going to follow me everywhere now?"

Jackson shrugged. "No idea. Most likely, if they

know your name, they'll end up staking out your apartment to get some candid shots. It wouldn't be a big deal if you lived somewhere with a doorman, but your place in China Town doesn't offer that kind of security."

"My apartment? Oh, this is terrible." Holly remembered how difficult it was to find her apartment in the first place. She couldn't imagine how she'd find a new one on her budget. Even with the raise she got from Jackson, she wouldn't have enough in her account for first and last month's rent as well as a deposit. And she wasn't sure what would come of leaving her lease early! She felt her stomach begin to churn.

"I know. It's completely uncalled for. I'll make a few calls and try to get the press to leave you alone. Until then, perhaps it would be best if you stayed with me."

Holly's eyes widened. She couldn't imagine that such close quarters would be good for their professional relationship. Things were slowly drifting into *Pretty Woman* territory whenever they were close and she could imagine crossing the line with Jackson if they lived together. "Stay with you? Like, at your apartment?"

He sat down in the chair beside hers, their knees almost touching. "The security there will keep the majority of those vultures away." He glanced in her direction and Holly could see by the pinched look on his face that things weren't going as he'd planned. "Of course, I have several guest rooms, so you would have total privacy. I don't want to make this any more uncomfortable for you than it already is. I really feel badly about it."

Holly reached down and placed a hand on his leg, trying to ignore the way her fingers burned. "Don't. It's not like you knew this would happen."

"No, but I should have been prepared for it. I know how the press is sometimes." He ran a hand through his thick hair. "We'll go now and move out some of your things before they find out where you live."

"But what about lunch with Ursula?"

"I'll call her in the car. She'll understand."

"Rick's downstairs waiting for her. How will we get to my place? I doubt we could get on the subway with all those photographers hounding us."

He pulled a set of keys out of his pocket. "No worries, I have a car. The garage opens up to a side street, so hopefully the reporters will still be out front."

***

Holly felt vaguely embarrassed as she unlocked the door to her apartment. Although she had brightened up the place with some artfully selected throw pillows and framed artwork, it was still a cramped apartment with peeling paint. Jackson, however, did not seem to notice and merely asked where her suitcases were kept.

"What should I bring? How long am I staying?" Her mind whirled as she led him to her bedroom, thankful that the bed was made, at least.

"I'm not sure, to be honest. At least until I can figure out how to keep the paparazzi away from you."

Holly unzipped a suitcase on her bed and began filling it with shoes and pairs of jeans. "The clothes you bought me are basically all in garment bags in the closet if you could get those for me. And I'm sorry for the mess. I didn't get a chance to tidy up."

"Mess?" Jackson furrowed his brow and looked around the room.

"My apartment," she elaborated, her face red. Surely the poverty simply wafted off the cheap, China Town apartment.

He shrugged and took off his suit jacket and tie. Holly looked away as he began to roll up his sleeves. It felt almost impure to see him in any state of undress, no matter how casual. Seeing him act in a way that wasn't his usual coiffed business persona flustered her, reminding her that he was still a man under all the designer suits—and a handsome man, at that.

"Mine would be worse if I didn't pay someone to pick up after me. Besides, I like your place. It has a very homey feel that most apartments don't have."

Holly smiled, trying to guess if he was joking or being serious. "You really think so?"

"Most definitely." He shot her a lopsided grin.

She tore her eyes away from him and went back to packing. "Are you sure me staying with you won't be an imposition?"

"You're the one doing me a favor by staying with me and pretending to be my fiancée. I'm the one messing up your life."

"Hardly. This is much more interesting than sitting at a desk and filing bank notes." She zipped up her suitcase, struggling to close it around all her clothes. "Nothing like this would ever happen in Michigan." Holly longed to call her mom and sister to tell them about all the ridiculous adventures she was having. She could imagine how they would brag to all the other islanders about the interesting life she led in New York City. But that would have to wait until Holly figured out what was going on. If the press found out they were faking their romance, her mom would be pretty pissed. She wouldn't want her oldest daughter lying.

"Did you hear that?" Jackson asked suddenly, looking toward the door. "I could have sworn I heard a knock. It better not be one of those reporters."

"Should we just pretend we're not here?"

Jackson squared his jaw and went through the living room. "No, I'll take care of them." He swung the door open. "What is it about 'no comment' don't you people understand? She's a private woman and deserves respect!"

"I-I'm sorry, I just wanted..." It was a female voice, and she sounded startled.

Holly thought she recognized it. "Amber? Is that you?"

Amber peeked her head around Jackson and smiled. "Hi, Holly."

Jackson frowned and looked back at Holly. "You know her?"

"Yes, she's my neighbor. You can let her in."

Amber came into the small living room, her gaze glued on Jackson. "I just wanted to see what all the commotion was about. I keep getting weird calls

63

from people asking to talk to you."

"I'm really sorry about that." Holly pulled her heavy suitcase toward the door and plopped it next to the chipping frame. "Those are just reporters. Keep telling them they have the wrong number and maybe they'll go away."

Her gaze shot toward Holly. "Reporters? Are you in some kind of trouble?"

"No. It's my fault," Jackson cut in. "Holly's now involved in my personal life and the press wants to know more about her."

"I guess it's because of campaign season, right?" Amber asked, looking around the room. "Holly, are you moving out?"

"Not exactly," she answered, piling some garment bags on top on her suitcase. She couldn't think of what to tell her.

Luckily, Jackson had an explanation for everything. "Holly and I had been talking about moving in together for a while, but all the reporters and the media are moving our timeline a bit."

"Wow, it's pretty crazy the reporters are basically pushing you out of your own home." Amber shook her head.

"Very much so," Jackson agreed. "And even though I'm willingly in the public eye, I want to spare Holly the stress. I would consider it a personal favor if you wouldn't mind ignoring the press for now, or answering any questions." He pulled a card out of his pocket and handed it to Amber. "This is my personal number. If anything happens, or the reporters won't leave, give me a call and I'll send someone over right away."

"I wouldn't say anything," Amber promised, going toward the door. "I'll let you get back to packing. Holly, call me soon, okay? Let me know how you're doing."

Holly nodded, zipping up the bag of toiletries she had brought from her tiny bathroom. "Yeah, I'll call you when things settle down a bit."

"All finished packing?" Jackson asked as Amber went into her apartment.

"Yeah, I think I have everything I need for now," she replied, looking around regretfully at her little home. Holly had worked long and hard to save up for the deposit and now, not even two weeks into living there, she was leaving.

"Good, let's get to my place."

***

"Here we are," Jackson said, opening up the front door and letting Holly inside. A bellboy followed, pushing a cart full of her garment bags and suitcases. The entryway was huge with high ceilings trimmed with elaborate crown molding and traditional wood furniture that looked as if it belonged in a museum. "Let me show you to your room so you can get settled in."

"Okay," Holly breathed, looking around her as they walked. Jackson watched her expression of awe out of the corner of his eye.

"Expecting something different?" he asked.

"Honestly? Yes. I thought it would be your basic bachelor pad with pizza boxes everywhere and a home theater."

"No, I had a decorator come in and ensure it was pizza-box-free. I do have a great home theater system, though." Jackson stopped at a door at the end of a long hallway and slowly opened it. "You can have this bedroom. It's only two doors from mine in case you need anything, at any time."

Holly gazed about the room and smiled, running a hand over the luscious bedspread. "This is lovely, thank you."

"It's the least I could do," he assured her, standing aside as a doorman came through carrying Holly's things. "Maybe it's better for you to stay here for the rest of our arrangement, anyway. I should have thought of it sooner."

"Because of the media?"

"And my mother. She would probably wonder why a couple in this day and age isn't living together. So, maybe this is for the best while she's visiting."

"I guess so."

"Do you need anything else?" He lingered in the doorway, subconsciously trying to think of a reason to stay. As he saw her standing in front of the bed, his mind created images of her bent over the brocade.

"No, I'm all right for now. I think I'll just unpack."

"Okay, make yourself at home. I'll have Mrs. Klein make something for dinner."

"Mrs. Klein?"

"The cook and housekeeper. She keeps this place fit for human life. If I was on my own, they'd condemn this place in a week."

66

The Non-Disclosure Agreement

Jackson closed Holly's bedroom door behind him and went off to find Mrs. Klein. The woman knew all the ins and outs of his life. And now he had to explain how she hadn't been informed about this new woman in his life.

***

After Jackson was gone and her clothes were put away in the walk-in closet, Holly felt her stomach growl. With all of the excitement of the day, she hadn't had any time to eat. She slipped out of her dress and pulled on a pair of leggings and a chunky Irish sweater before taking off her makeup. She liked dressing up and playing the role of fancy socialite, but sometimes it was nicer to be her old self again.

She quietly opened her bedroom door and looked up and down the long hallway. The apartment was quiet, but she could smell something delicious. Holly padded down the corridor, following the scents, and came to the kitchen. It was an extremely modern room with stainless steel appliances where a portly woman flitted about pulling pans from the oven and stirring pots.

"Excuse me," Holly said.

The cook turned on her heel and looked at Holly in surprise. "Oh, bless you! You must be Miss McIntyre, the lady of the house!"

Holly giggled at the thought of being considered the lady of the house. "And you must be Mrs. Klein. Please call me Holly."

Mrs. Klein crossed the kitchen and threw her

arms around Holly's waist. "When Mr. Cantrell told me his fiancée was moving in, I could barely believe it! The boy is finally going to have a little love nest!" She stepped back and looked Holly up and down, her chocolate eyes sparkling. "And such a pretty young thing you are."

"Thank you, ma'am."

Mrs. Klein let go of Holly and turned back to the stove after patting her gray bun back into place. "I hope you're hungry. As soon as Mr. Cantrell told me you were doing some moving, I knew you would work up a healthy appetite."

"Starving. Everything smells delicious."

"Oh, a girl who eats! Bless your heart. All those little chickies who are too afraid to have a good meal! There's more to food than just salads and fruits."

"Is there anything I can do to help?"

"Oh, no." She shook her head. "I have everything all set, dear. The food will be served in a few moments if you'd like to go tell Mr. Cantrell."

"Is he still here? I thought he might have gone back to work."

"He should be in his office. It's the third door down the hall."

Holly backed out of the room and looked at the row of doors down the long hallway. She counted three doors down and gently knocked. "Jackson, are you in there?" There was no response. She tapped again before opening it, wondering if she had been knocking on the door of a linen closet. She was greeted by Jackson's muscular, shirtless body.

He was doing pushups and wearing a pair of

headphones blasting music, so he hadn't heard her. It was his home gym she'd walked into, not his office. Holly stood there, staring, watching his naked arms push his taut body up. His tanned back flexed as he exercised, his skin gleaming with fresh sweat. She bit her lip, unsure of what to do and unable to take her eyes away from him. He was hard in all the right places and she thought it was a damn shame he always hid such an amazing physique under suits and ties. But if he was always half-naked in the privacy of his own home, she thought she might enjoy living with him after all.

Jackson glanced up momentarily and caught her staring at him. "Oh, hello." He stopped his workout and smiled up at her, pulling off his headphones.

"Um, hi," she whispered, her face burning. Even with him looking right at her, she couldn't tear her gaze away from the strong indent of his spine and broad shoulder blades. "I knocked."

"Sorry, I always do a little bit of exercise at some point during the day." He stood up, giving Holly a good look at his chest and abs, both as attractive as the backside.

"It's okay," she answered, her eyes fixed on his sculpted torso.

"Is everything all right?"

"Mrs. Klein said it was time to eat."

"Great." He grabbed a shirt off his bed and followed her into the hallway.

As he pulled it over his head, she couldn't help but think it was a pity for him to cover up. She was looking forward to a show with her dinner. But she couldn't complain too much about it. He looked so casual in a pair of athletic shorts. It was such a stark contrast to the usual business attire she always saw him in and she rather liked the change. "Sorry about bursting in like that. I thought that was your office."

"My office is a few doors over," he explained, pulling on his t-shirt. "It's the room between our bedrooms."

"Mr. Cantrell!" Mrs. Klein had set the table in the dining room and had several covered dishes spread on the long mahogany table. "I've made a bit of a feast for you two love birds." She shuffled them both into seats on either side of the table. "Where have you been hiding Miss Holly all this time?"

"Michigan," he answered, lifting the covers off the food to reveal roasted chicken, mashed potatoes, salad, corn, cranberry sauce, rolls, and green beans. "This looks great, Mrs. Klein, thank you."

"Of course! Anything for the cute couple!" She flew back into the kitchen.

"She's very nice," Holly noted, taking a spoonful of mashed potatoes and plopping it onto her gold trimmed plate. Her mouth watered as she piled her plate high with a bit of everything.

"She seems to like you." Jackson groaned as he took a bite of his chicken. "I'm telling you, if she was thirty years younger, single, and could still cook like this, I'd have to hire her as my fake fiancée and you'd be out of a job."

Holly giggled and took a bite of corn. "It is delicious, so I couldn't even be mad."

"I like that sound."

"What sound?"

"Your laugh. I don't think I've ever really heard it before."

Her cheeks warmed. She wasn't used to being complimented, but hearing it come from Jackson made it almost harder to take in. "I laugh all the time. I'm just usually more reserved when I'm at work or with your mother."

"Why?"

"Because that's my job, isn't it? To be the perfect society woman?"

"You're still allowed to laugh in society."

"It doesn't look that way."

He frowned. "Well I think you should be less reserved. I mean, right now I see a different side of you."

"What do you mean?"

He took a swig of the red wine Mrs. Klein had left for them. "Before our proposal began, you dressed sensibly and couldn't even look me in the eye. Once you became my fiancée-for-hire, you became a society woman. Today, for example, you looked like a 5th Avenue goddess—perfect hair, makeup, shoes, dress. And you seemed to have the confidence to match. You looked great before, don't get me wrong, but right now I'm just seeing a different side of you."

"The lazy side?" she asked with amusement, pointing toward her bulky sweater. "You're one to talk." She pointed at his t-shirt.

"No, the real side. You looked amazing today when you came to my office, but I think I like this you more. No makeup and laughing at everything," he explained. "I'm around depressed people all day long. My job is to basically buy out companies and make people miserable. I would hate to think that I'm making you uncomfortable, as well, when you've done so much to help me in my time of need."

"I guess I feel weird relaxing around you," Holly confessed, looking down at her food. "To me, you're still my boss."

"True. But, please don't feel the need to be prim and proper around me at all times, especially here at the apartment. I want you to be comfortable since I've taken you out of your home."

"Don't feel bad. It's not much of a home, anyway." She tried to sound nonchalant, but she rather missed her little hole away from the world. Although, she did think she could get used to the hotel-like accommodations. Especially if Jackson always forwent his intimidating suits at home.

"And why is that?"

"It's just so empty. I don't really like feeling like I'm alone, and being in a quiet apartment by myself is just a reminder of how few people I know here. Back in Michigan, I was always down in my parents' restaurant or home with my loud-mouthed little sister." Holly drifted off, suddenly missing her family. She felt her throat grow tight and took a sip of wine to try to loosen it up.

Jackson nodded. "I understand."

"How? You're surrounded by people all day and you've lived here your whole life."

"True. But even in a crowded room you can feel alone when you're among strangers and people who only want your money."

She peered at him from under her lashes. His candid honesty appealed to her. This icy god had a soul after all. "I guess I never thought of it that way."

"Do you really feel alone here, Holly?"

She paused for just a moment. "Very. I only know you and your mother, now, Amber, and a few people who work for you."

He seemed surprised by her answer. "Do you think that's why you wanted a dog?"

"I suppose that's part of it. Companionship, love, a pet to take for walks through Central Park, all that fun stuff."

"Why? It's not like Central Park is all that great," Jackson mumbled, his mouth full of mashed potatoes.

"Oh, that's attractive," Holly teased. "I've always wondered what my boss would look like talking with masticated potato in his mouth."

"I live to make your dreams come true," he answered smartly.

Their gazes met for a moment and Holly's stomach flipped. The casual conversation they shared really put her at ease. She took her gaze away and asked, "Is Central Park really not what it looks like on TV and in movies?"

He furrowed his brow, his mouth set in a firm line. "You've never been?"

"No, I keep meaning to go, but haven't found the time yet."

"Well then, are you up for a little adventure?"

***

Ten minutes later, they were riding the elevator downstairs to go see Central Park. As soon as Jackson suggested it, Holly ran to her room and pulled on riding-style boots and a pair of big sunglasses. Her excitement was palpable and as soon as she tore from the dining room, Jackson changed into a pair of well-worn jeans and a casual button-down with the sleeves rolled up.

Jackson thought it was the perfect time for a walk outside in the dusky light. Fall was just beginning, so the air was slightly crisp and the leaves were just beginning to turn shades of yellow and gold. The sidewalk was empty of the dreaded paparazzi and no one gave them a second glance as they strolled toward the iron gates and tree-lined paths.

"Where else haven't you been?" Jackson asked. He always forgot that while New York City was his home, to others it was a tourist destination.

"Everywhere. This is the first time I've been so far away from home."

He raised his eyebrows in surprise. "You're telling me you've never left Michigan?"

"Well, I've been to Ohio and Canada, but never anywhere else. My family never really had the time or the money to do vacations."

"If you could go somewhere, where would it be?" He wondered what kind of vacation spot Holly would pick. The ancient cities of Greece? Or would she want to walk the white beaches of Barbados? Jackson could imagine her in a barely-there bikini, which would be worth taking the Cantrell International jet for a little spin.

"Anywhere, really," she answered, her gaze darting around her at the horse-drawn carriages and vendors selling snacks and artwork.

"There isn't anywhere in particular you've had in mind? Somewhere you've always wanted to go?" *Please say Barbados.*

"It was New York City, but here I am. I guess I need to find a new destination."

"Is it all you thought it would be?"

"Well, I've been here less than two weeks and I have a rich fiancé who has nice hair, a closet full of designer clothes, an apartment that overlooks Central Park, and a staff to cook, clean, and manicure me. I think I'm doing quite well," she joked.

Jackson ran a hand through his thick black hair and shot her a grin. "You really think my hair is nice?"

Holly laughed and playfully shoved him. "You know you have nice hair. You don't need your assistant reminding you, so you go and get a big head."

"Now, now, isn't that why I made you my fiancée? Assistants are for fetching coffee and filing paperwork," he said with a dignified air, thoroughly enjoying their game. "Fiancées are for boosting egos."

"Oh, so clearly I'm in the wrong line of work. I certainly don't fawn over you enough."

"I'm glad you don't."

"And why's that?" Holly asked, stopping to pet the neck of a dappled gray carriage horse.

"I have people fawning over me all the time.

People want jobs, women want dates, everyone trips over themselves trying to get me to notice them."

"Must be strange."

He shrugged. "Maybe it is. It must be how you feel sometimes. Gentlemen callers knocking down your door and professing their love to you with bunches of flowers."

Holly held up her hand with the diamond ring firmly in place. "Well, good sir, it would hardly be proper of me to worry about men asking me on dates when I am clearly in a deeply committed relationship."

Jackson uttered a deep, rich laugh that was slightly dusty with disuse. He couldn't remember the last time he'd genuinely laughed. It was nice. And even nicer knowing he didn't have any competition, not that he had any right to her. "Very true. It wouldn't be proper at all."

They walked that way in silence for a while, their hands accidentally brushing a dozen times before Jackson grabbed her frozen one in his own warm one, their fingers interlocked in a strange, yet comfortable way. As soon as his palm touched hers, he thought Holly might pull away. But he was pleased when the gesture didn't seem to bother her. To any other person in the park, they would look like a normal couple strolling in the sunset.

Being like this with Holly felt so natural that, for a brief moment, he almost forgot who she was— who *he* was. While he knew he was merely pretending, a part of him wished he didn't have to. Part of him wished it wasn't just a game. But so far, no one would ever guess Jackson was a lonely businessman who'd hired Holly to be his fiancée in order to win the Republican ticket.

***

Holly woke early the next morning to her cellphone ringing loudly, inches from her face. She was exhausted after coming back last night from her little adventure with Jackson. They walked through the entire park and even took a stroll through the Central Park zoo. He had noticed how she fawned over the cuddly red pandas in one exhibit, cooing over the way they dashed about their enclosure. He had bought her a small, stuffed version. When she didn't immediately accept, Jackson basically forced her to take it. He had said that it wasn't a real New York excursion without a souvenir. The little animal now sat on the other side of the bed, a pleasant reminder of their evening.

Best of all, Jackson did not let go of her hand until they were back in the apartment where he wished her goodnight with a smile and headed into his own bedroom. Holly's hand felt almost naked and she briefly longed for the warm closeness of his grip.

She slid the iPhone open groggily, not bothering to look at the screen. "Hello?"

"Oh, Holly!" It was her mother. "You're in the magazine!"

Holly rubbed her eyes and looked at the alarm clock on the nightstand. It was only seven in the morning. She was almost regretting giving her mother her new phone number. "What are you talking about, Mom?"

"I was flipping through one of those celebrity news magazines when they came in this morning, and there you were!"

Still confused, Holly sat up and stretched, trying to wake herself up. Considering how plush and decadent the bed was, it wasn't an easy task. "Where was I?"

"In. The. Magazine," Janice answered, her voice showing her exasperation. "Honestly, dear, you need to listen more. You were there in the magazine wearing a lovely dress and it said under the picture that you were the 'mysterious beauty who stole the billionaire's heart.' Isn't that just crazy? They didn't know your name, but I would know my baby girl anywhere."

"And you're sure it was me?"

Her mother let out a huff. "Of course it was you! They had you next to that man you're working for…Jason Catskill? Josh Carlton? Is that the man you're dating? The guy running for mayor?"

Holly paled. There was no way she was in a magazine! "Jackson Cantrell?"

"Oh, that's it. So it's true, then? They're calling you mysterious and stunning! My baby is mysterious and stunning and has a boyfriend! Isn't that something? Is he coming for Christmas? He would really spice up our Christmas card. And think of how jealous the other ladies at knitting circle would be!"

"What magazine was this?" she asked, ignoring mom's constant blabbering.

"Oh, I don't know. You were in a few I think.

The whole island's going to be talking about it. You're going to be quite the little celebrity back home."

Holly flopped back into the soft pillows, suddenly feeling ill. "There's more than one?"

"Yes, I'm looking through another now." Holly could hear the rustling of papers. "Oh, here you are! Goodness, isn't he a handsome one? You look good too, dear. How romantic."

"What is it?"

"A picture of you and that Jackson fellow in a park holding hands. That's so sweet! Why didn't you tell us about him before? You know your sister found these pictures first. She's the one who reads this garbage. Your father wants to know more about this boy. I tried to use the Google to look him up, but I can't put any words in. I think my Google is on the fritz, so I have to wait to use the Internets to look you up. Mrs. Heigel next door says that she saw you on the television too, but she couldn't find a tape to record it on her VCR." She paused to take a breath. "Why didn't you tell me you had a boyfriend?"

"I-I don't know...it all happened so fast." Holly felt a pang of guilt at lying to her mother. They always had a relationship full of honesty, but the ironclad non-disclosure agreement meant she couldn't say anything.

"Well, this picture shows you coming out of some place together...his apartment, apparently!" Janice gasped. "Holly, now the whole town will think you've run away from Michigan and jumped into bed with a stranger in New York!"

"It's not like that, Mom. We just ate dinner. That's all. Jackson's rather old-fashioned. I mean, we're practically engaged," she told her wryly, darkly amused by her own little joke. "I need to go tell Jackson that we're in the magazines. I'll call you later."

Once she got her mother off the phone, she wondered if he would be awake yet. While she hated to potentially ruin his sleep, she knew he'd want to know this new information right away. Holly stepped into the bathroom to brush her teeth and look at herself in the mirror, before straightening her yoga pants and tank top and going down the hall to Jackson's room. She hadn't seen inside, and wondered what it would be like. But, more than anything, Holly was nervous. It seemed oddly intimate to be going into his more personal space. But he needed to hear about the tabloids from her before he left for the office. She lightly knocked on the door and opened it slowly when she heard him say, "Come in."

"Jackson—"

Again, he was shirtless, but now he was fresh out of the shower and wearing a towel. Context clues told her there was nothing underneath. She bit the inside of her cheek, willing her jaw to not fall open. One layer of fabric was the only thing keeping her from seeing him—*all* of him.

"Yes?" He seemed unaffected by being caught almost nude by his fake fiancée.

"Um, I..." She turned her gaze to the floor to keep from being rendered completely speechless by the view. "My mother just called me. There are

80

pictures of us in the celebrity magazines."

"Damn. I'm sorry about that, Holly. I thought they didn't get any good shots of the two of us together."

"They had some from the park last night." Her eyes betrayed her and snaked up his legs, over his abs, settling on his freshly shaved face.

"Really? I didn't even see them." He ran his hands through his damp hair, tousling the tendrils.

"Yeah. I guess my whole town's going to think I'm dating some rich city boy now."

"Did you tell your mother about our arrangement?"

She shook her head. "No, of course not. I think she's actually pleased I finally landed a man."

"Good. I can't take any chances. I just didn't know this would get so far out of hand so quickly. I thought I had some time."

Holly knew she needed to excuse herself from his presence. The sight of him was far too intimate for their professional arrangement. "I think I'm going to go downstairs and see if I can find a newsstand that sells magazines so I can see for myself."

"That's a really good idea," he said, crossing over to a large dresser in the corner. He opened a drawer and pulled out a single key on a ring. "Here's a key for the apartment. I've already put you on the list, so getting inside the lobby won't be a problem. This key is for the elevator door that leads up to our floor. Would you like me to send someone out for magazines?"

"No, I think I'd like to go out by myself." Holly

took the key from his hand, admiring how quickly her boss got things done. "Are you going somewhere?"

He looked at her quizzically. "Work. It's only Thursday."

"Oh, I forgot," she admitted sheepishly. She had gone into his room, fully aware that it was a weekday, but her mind had melted the longer they spoke.

"Being a lady of leisure already has your days all mixed up," he teased, stepping into his walk-in closet. "Don't forget my mother's coming here for lunch today. Just be your usual, charming self."

"Do you think she has seen the tabloids yet?" Holly asked nervously, stepping a bit to the side to watch him.

He shrugged and flipped through his suits until he selected a dark charcoal colored one. "One of her assistants probably gave her the highlights. Can you pick a shirt and tie to go with this? I need to finish getting ready for work."

Holly stepped into the closet as Jackson went to his own bathroom and closed the door behind him. She looked at the racks of perfectly pressed clothes and was stunned at the numbers of suits and dress shirts he owned. He had enough to outfit every man in her town three times over. She pulled a pale blue shirt off the rack and a dove gray tie to go with it. The blue of the shirt would emphasize his eyes. It felt oddly intimate to be picking out Jackson's clothes for the day. She recalled how her mother had always picked out her father's clothes when they were going out to dinner or a party with friends. But, on the other hand, Holly was Jackson's assistant and getting whatever her boss needed was part of her job description.

She placed the outfit on his bed and went to her room to change her own clothes. After a quick shower, Holly dressed in a pair of jeans and a plain black blouse. She pulled her wet hair into a bun and put on a pair of bug-eyed sunglasses to hide her face. Lastly, she donned a comfortable pair of black flats and grabbed her purse and new key before going downstairs. She did not want anyone to see her and recognize her.

Thankfully, the streets were still fairly quiet, empty, and seemingly free of photographers. The only people on the sidewalks were men and women in business suits who weren't interested in her at all. Holly walked a block before she found a newsstand that carried everything from the New York Times to The National Enquirer. She picked up every magazine in sight and scurried back to the apartment.

Once she was back in the safety of the high-rise, she sat in her temporary bedroom on top of the giant bed. It was freshly made, so she assumed Mrs. Klein had been in to tidy up. She could hear her cooking in the kitchen, banging pots and pans about, and she wondered briefly if Jackson was still in the apartment. If it weren't for the pile of tempting tabloids in front of her, she might have gone looking for him.

Holly kicked off her shoes and plopped on the bed before she opened the first magazine. She flipped through until she saw a full-page picture of herself with the title

The Blonde Bombshell and the Billionaire.

What her mother told her was true. There she was in full color, her hair flawlessly waved and her face smooth and brightened thanks to her recent spa trip and her fancy new makeup. Her purple dress cut her figure perfectly and made her look effortlessly fashionable. It hardly even looked like her. But the face in the photo had a look of perfect surprise that made her seem like a model in a print ad for sunscreen. The giant engagement ring she now wore was hidden in this photo by Jackson's suit jacket. She was momentarily grateful that the press didn't see her as a fiancée. She could only imagine how crazy the media would be then.

On the next page, she found the article.

Gasp! Say it's not so! New York's most eligible (and tasty) billionaire Jackson Cantrell has been taken off the market by a mysterious blonde. Just in time for campaign season, Cantrell seems to intend to debut a new wife, as well as some new city ordinances. Although she is still unnamed, she has already been spotted all over the city with our favorite gorgeous man. She even met his mother, the beautiful ex-model and designer Ursula Gaspar-Cantrell.

Their romance is apparently still fresh and new, but she is the first girl Cantrell has dated who doesn't have any ties in the acting or modeling world. Or at least none we know of.

Here she is (Pictured on page 22) looking glamorous and poised outside of Cantrell International. While our photographers caught her by surprise, she still looked stunning as she rushed inside the building for some afternoon delight. A source close to the couple told us, "Jackson's head over heels in love with his new girlfriend and has even introduced her to his family. Everyone who knows him wouldn't be surprised if they got married or pregnant really soon. They're that much in love!" You heard it here, ladies and gentleman. Jackson Cantrell is taken!

Holly rolled her eyes and tossed the magazine aside. She didn't understand why she was so interesting to those people. Surely, there was some celebrity in rehab they could be writing about instead of her. But it was strange to know that she was the first girl Jackson has been linked to who wasn't famous. And at least the magazines weren't rude in their dissection of her.

The next magazine featured a story about her as well. They printed pictures of her and Jackson at the park holding hands, playfully pushing each other, looking like a couple in love. The article was titled:

Fresh-Faced Beauty Snags her Real Life Prince Charming.

Reports have been pouring in about business

85

tycoon Jackson Cantrell and his newest love interest. While we are still working on securing a name for the most current girlfriend, we have secured several adorable shots that show Cantrell in an all new light. Usually so reserved and dignified, Cantrell was spotted taking a leisurely stroll in Central Park with his new ladylove in a casual outfit of jeans and button-down (Ralph Lauren). The blonde was wearing a pair of riding boots and a knitted sweater of unknown designs.

His fresh-faced girlfriend brought out the playful side of Cantrell as they were seen petting the park's horses and laughing at jokes. While this girl does not fit his usual type of willow-thin brunette, it doesn't look like this curvy blonde beauty will be going anywhere any time soon. The possible future Mayor of New York City's First Lady might be the most beautiful one yet.

Holly paused. She didn't know that Jackson always dated brunettes. In fact, he once told her that he preferred blondes. Of course, he was probably just saying anything at that point to get her to agree to his plan. She was about to open another when a sharp knock interrupted her musings.

"Who is it?"

"It's Jackson. Can I come in?" The door muffled his voice.

"Yes, of course," she called back, tiding up the stack of magazines.

Jackson entered wearing the outfit Holly had laid aside for him and she was pleased to see the colors worked perfectly. He sat down on the edge of the bed and ran a hand through his hair, inspecting the magazines. "So, what are they saying?"

"Basically that I'm a blonde is a total surprise to them, you're terribly desired by everyone, we are desperately in love, and that we'll probably have a baby out of wedlock soon since you're apparently so ready to add to the Cantrell family line."

He laughed. "Oh, is that all?

"Basically, but I've only looked at a few, so who knows what else I'll learn about us."

"Was your family upset?"

"No. They see me as a bit of a celebrity. I think my mom's pretty pleased about having me in the magazines. Our neighbor has a daughter who's a doctor, so I think my mom's excited to have a bit of prestige among her children. It'll be pretty weird to pretend we're dating to my parents. They hate lying and wouldn't understand your point of view, so I'll just have to invent a breakup eventually."

"I'm sorry this is getting so much publicity. If this hadn't gone in the magazines, you wouldn't have to lie to your family." He looked genuinely remorseful.

"It's okay. The paparazzi don't even know my name and they don't know about the engagement, so it's not that bad. At least I look good in the pictures."

"You always look good," Jackson said, rising and fixing his tie.

Holly blushed. "Thanks."

"Stop getting so embarrassed," Jackson admonished with a grin. "I wouldn't get engaged to any woman who wasn't absolutely stunning. Even the magazines say so."

Her cheeks grew a deeper shade of crimson. "You're such a suck-up." She reached beside her and picked up a gold throw pillow. She chucked it at him, but he caught it easily and threw it on the foot of the bed.

"Guilty as charged. Now, I need to go in to the office for a few meetings. Mother is coming at noon for lunch, so Mrs. Klein will take care of all the food. All you need to do is keep being charming."

"Okay. Is there anything else I can do for you?"

"Holly, you're not my assistant anymore. You need to act like my fiancée even when you think no one's around. I can't have my mother know this is all a lie."

"Okay, I'll try to pretend to be madly in love with you like the magazines say."

"That's my girl." Jackson winked at her as he left and closed the door behind him.

Holly sighed and flopped back on her fluffy pillows. It was so weird to be Jackson's fake fiancée. There was nothing at all for her to do all day but have lunch with Ursula, and even then it wasn't as if she was cooking. The life of a socialite was a little too boring.

***

At noon, a deep chime announced Ursula's arrival. Holly smoothed out her navy sundress and opened the front door. "Good afternoon, Ursula."

"Holly, darling." She greeted her with a hovering

kiss above her cheeks in the European fashion.

"Would you like something to drink?" Holly asked as she led Ursula to the dining room. It felt odd playing the hostess in someone else's home, but she knew she had to push through and at least *look* comfortable in her role.

"Red wine. It keeps me young." She dropped her large purse on the table with a thump.

Holly poured them each a small glass as Mrs. Klein began serving their lunch of spinach salad, stuffed red peppers, and grilled chicken. "How long are you staying in New York?"

"I do not know. Now that Jackson has decided to settle down, I want to be close to him and get to know you better," Ursula told her in lightly accented French. Her pale blue eyes peered around the apartment. "I haven't been in this apartment in so long. It seems to be completely unchanged."

"Should it have been?" Holly asked, taking a bit of salad.

"Well, now that a woman is living here, I thought it would have more of a homey feel. This place still feels like a hotel."

"That's just what I thought when I first saw it," she admitted. "But I guess I also expected it to be more modern and look more like a bachelor pad."

"Jackson has always had an old soul. He's very traditional. I suppose that's why I was surprised to meet you and also surprised it had taken him so long."

"He's only twenty-six." Holly wondered if Ursula thought of her as an old maid at twenty-four.

"Yes, but he wasted all that time with those

flighty women who offered nothing."

"Offered nothing?"

"They had no breeding, no taste, no real aspirations other than getting my son's money. All they did was work as hangers for clothes."

Holly fought a smile at her words. If she was correct, Ursula used to be a model herself, who married a much older and much richer man. "So you never approved of any of them?"

Ursula laughed. "Approved? When a vapid woman who eats less than a bird runs about New York City spending your son's money, it is hard to approve."

Holly bit her lip. Ursula was more critical of Jackson's girlfriends than she would have ever dreamed. "I understand."

Ursula studied her, swirling her glass of wine. "Do I make you nervous?"

"Nervous?"

"Yes. Nervous."

"A bit. You're Jackson's mom and I don't want you to dislike me."

"What's not to like? You are pretty, a good conversationalist, have the right kind of breeding, and according to the tabloids, you make my son quite happy."

"So you've seen those?" Holly asked, her eyes downturned. It was so embarrassing to think that Jackson's mother had read all of those ridiculous articles gushing about how in love they were.

"Obviously. I have my assistant go through all of the tabloids to see if anything about my son or myself is printed. If it is good, I ignore it. If it is bad and potentially damaging to our images or the company, then I alert my lawyers."

Holly suppressed a laugh. If only Ursula knew what her son asked *his* assistant to do. "I read them this morning."

"I was brought a few of the more interesting ones. They were all the usual rubbish, but they had several nice photographs of the two of you at the park. It is nice to see Jackson have a little fun now and then. He has always been serious. Even as a child." Ursula poured herself another glass of wine and kept her icy stare trained on Holly. "I think you are a good influence on him."

"Thank you."

"But I am curious, how long have you been seeing my son?"

She was taken aback by Ursula's question. She and Jackson never spoke about the beginnings of their relationship. "Well…it's hard to say…not that long."

"Whirlwind romance?"

"You could call it that."

"And you would say you know my son well?"

"You can never know the person you're with enough, and we both have a lot to learn," Holly answered vaguely, hoping the line of conversation would die off.

"Holly, do you have any idea how much my son is worth? How much he makes a year?"

"Honestly? I never asked. I assumed it was a lot, but I was taught to never discuss finances with anyone."

"So you plan on keeping your finances separate

until after you're married?" Ursula raised a perfectly sculpted eyebrow.

"Jackson and I haven't really discussed that yet. I mean, it's not like we're getting married anytime soon."

"Why not?"

"Why not, what?"

"Why are you planning on having a long engagement?"

The questioning was starting to get to her. Holly felt her poised demeanor crack under the pressure of Ursula's gaze. "We feel that these things shouldn't be rushed and that it's important to live together before making such a big commitment." Holly was proud of her answer. It sounded both responsible and appropriate.

"And then there will be children?"

Holly almost spit her mouthful of wine all over the table. "Ch-children?"

"Obviously. He has always said he wanted two or three."

"Well, I guess when the time comes, we can discuss that."

After an awkward pause, Ursula broke the silence. "You know, I never went to college either. I was much too interested in starting my life." Ursula waved her pale hands in front of her face. "Who needs a degree when you have talent and aspirations? Women like us would only be stifled by classrooms."

"Women like us?"

"*Artistic* women. There are far too few of us left in the world and that, my dear, is a terrible shame."

She reached into her purse and pulled out a thick binder. "Now, let us discuss this wedding. I have some ideas I think you will like."

***

"Honey, I'm home," Jackson called from the entryway.

Holly laughed and came down the hall to greet him, "Hi, how was work?"

"Fine. Closed a few deals, so that was a load off. I also have a meeting set up to talk to Denny about how to market our relationship." He placed his briefcase on a table next to the front door and looked her up and down. "Did you wear that to meet my mother?"

Holly looked down at her sundress and frowned. "What's wrong with it?"

"Nothing at all. I like it. How was she?" Jackson loosened his tie and pulled his jacket from his shoulders.

"She was…curious."

He raised an eyebrow, reminding Holly of his mother. "Curious, you say?"

"She wanted to know our plans and when we were getting married."

"What did you tell her?"

"I made up some things about needing to make sure we were right for each other and that we've been so caught up in getting engaged that we haven't really discussed anything like joining finances."

"So we're still the picture of new love?"

Kelsey McKnight

"As far as she's concerned, yes."

He grinned and placed a hand on her shoulder. "Perfect. You did really well. I hope she didn't scare you."

The place where their skin touched burned and she hoped the heat didn't meet her face. "No, she's a little intimidating, but I think she likes me."

"Good, good. Is Mrs. Klein making dinner yet?" He took his hand back and walked toward the kitchen. "It smells great in here and I'm seriously starving."

"Actually, I gave Mrs. Klein the night off," Holly confessed.

He stopped and turned to look at her in confusion. "Why?"

"She looked tired and I thought she should go to her room and rest. I'm cooking dinner."

Jackson grinned. "So I'm marrying a girl who can cook? Perfect. I'll go change and see how good of a chef you are."

Holly watched him go into his room and she returned to the high tech kitchen. She was making fettuccini alfredo with garlic bread. It was simple, but it was a dish she knew she could cook well. For a moment she imagined what it would feel like if all of this were real.

Holly knew she was just getting paid to play the part of a loving fiancée, but she almost wished it were true. It felt so comfortable and right that they'd be together like this. But Jackson dated sophisticated brunette supermodels, while she was an average girl from Michigan who just happened to be hired as his personal assistant. She did not belong in this penthouse apartment wearing expensive shoes and pretending to be engaged to the devastatingly handsome billionaire.

Sighing, Holly poured herself a glass of wine and began plating their meal. She started feeling terribly inadequate and suddenly her pathetic attempt at playing house made her feel ill. Now the once deliciously fragrant pasta turned her stomach, the garlic bread looked soggy, and the entire dinner seemed like a disaster.

She downed a few gulps of wine and filled the glass up again. Jackson could be heard whistling in the adjoining dining room. Even though she could not place the tune, she knew he sounded happy.

"What's for dinner?" Jackson interrupted her thoughts, popping his head in the kitchen.

"Just some pasta and garlic bread. Nothing crazy," she said, turning to meet him, hoping to hide the shame she was trying to push down with a little more wine.

He came in the room and took the two full plates. "Let me help you with these."

Holly followed him into the dining room with her wine glass in hand. Already she felt her the alcohol making her mind fuzzy. Brushing off her unease, she sat on the other side of the table from Jackson, who was looking up at her with a smile.

"Why are you looking at me like that?" she asked, her cheeks red.

"I was just thinking that I couldn't have picked anyone better to do this with."

"I was just in the right place at the right time," Holly mumbled, taking another sip of her wine.

"No, I mean it. I thought this would be all business, but to be honest I rather like having you around."

Holly blushed and put down her wine glass to hide her trembling hands. Her heart started fluttering, the wine adding to the frantic beating. It took a moment before she found herself able to speak. "What do you mean?"

"I'm just glad that we ended up being friends, you know? It would be unfortunate to be stuck in this position with someone I didn't get along with. I like that this doesn't feel awkward and forced."

Holly felt a pang in her chest. He just saw her as a friend. She knew she should have never hoped for more. "Yeah, that would be terrible."

"Hey, are you okay?" His brows furrowed. "Do you feel all right?"

She shot her head up and gave him a smile. "Yes, of course. Just a little too much wine today."

"Are you sure?"

"Why wouldn't I be?"

"No reason." He took a bit of his pasta and gave a moan of satisfaction. "This pasta is the best. You're a natural cook."

"I try," she said, drinking a bit more wine. She poked at the noodles with her fork, but found she wasn't all that hungry.

"You know, you said you had too much wine. Are you sure you should keep drinking?"

"What can I say? I like to live dangerously." She smirked, reaching for the bottle. The wine filled her glass and she hoped it would fill the aching void within her as well.

He laughed in between bites. "You know, tomorrow night there's this charity dinner I have to go to. It'll be exceedingly boring and attended by dozens of people I'll need to trick into thinking I'm the best man for mayor. Would you like to come with me?"

"Yes, of course. What time?"

"We'll leave here a bit before eight. It's at the Museum of Modern Art."

Her heart quickened and her eyes widened in excitement at the mention of a place on her list of places to visit. "Really? I haven't had a chance to go there either."

"Well, now you'll be able to explore the whole place without the packs of tourists roaming around."

Holly drank some more wine, noting how she hardly tasted its deep, earthy notes anymore. "So, I can't have a personal tour like a fancy tourist?"

"No. You have a full time address here, and after tomorrow night, you'll know all the major players in this city. After that, you can hardly be considered a tourist. But we'll see what we can do about a tour."

She raised her brows, impressed. Jackson certainly worked fast. "What should I wear?"

"It's a formal event so you'll need to get a floor-length dress."

"More shopping?" She sighed. Although she could put a nice outfit together, picking the pieces out of the store was what she found difficult.

"But of course. Go to Nordstrom and put it on my account."

She traced the rim of her glass with one finger.

"Does it bother you? Spending money on me like this?"

He looked surprised. "Why would it bother me? I'm *asking* you to do these things. I *need* you to do these things. I'm practically begging you to spend my money."

"Women's clothes are expensive here," Holly mumbled as she took another sip. "In Michigan, no one ever went shopping like this. Here, it's all the women do."

"Does shopping really bother you that much?"

She shook her head, noting how the room kept moving although her head had stopped. "No, no, no. I like to shop. Shop…it's a weird word. *Shop…*"

The corners of his mouth turned into a dimpled grin. "Holly, are you drunk?"

She started to take another sip of wine only to find that it was all gone. She could not remember finishing her glass, but as she thought about how much she drank, she began to feel dizzy. In her nervousness this evening, she'd drank far too much, eaten too little, and she'd pay for it in the morning.

"Holly? Holly?" Jackson's voice suddenly sounded far away.

"Hi, Jackson," she slurred as he came into vision. Holly studied his face, giggling as his smiling lips came into focus. She didn't think she had been that drunk since she and her ex-boyfriend had stolen an entire bottle of vodka from the bar at her parents' restaurant as teenagers.

"You're seriously drunk?" He laughed. "How much did you drink?"

She pointed at the glass then held up two fingers,

then three, then she gave up. "Too many."

He got up from his chair and came over to her side of the table. "I think it's time for bed, missy."

"No. I have energy. Let's stay up!" She grinned up at him.

Jackson looked at her, thoroughly amused. "And what do you want to do with all of your energy?"

"I don't know," she said, slowly standing in a way she hoped was graceful. "I can think of a few things." Holly made a grab for Jackson, missing him by an inch. She fell down on her knees and struggled to get back on her high-heeled feet.

"Whoa!" Jackson held out his hands and pulled her up, holding her against him. "It's definitely time to put you to bed."

"*You* go to bed!" She let loose a shriek-like giggle as she grabbed his loosened tie and yanked it over his head.

Chuckling, Jackson lifted her up in his arms and carried her bridal-style into her bedroom and placed her gently on her bed. He slipped off her pumps and placed them quietly on the floor. Then he pulled down the covers and tried to slide her between the sheets.

"Are you trying to get rid of me?" Holly's words were jumbled together and she suddenly felt as if her dress was too constricting. "I wanna stay up! I have energy!"

"No, Holly, I'm just trying to put you in bed so you can sleep this off. You have a lot of shopping to do in the morning."

"I don't *want* to go shopping." Holly pouted and sat up, grabbing the hem of her skirt. "Stay in bed with me," she said, stripping her dress off over her head and throwing it on the floor next to her shoes. She was left in a pale blue lace bra and matching panties. Holly felt her body temperature rise as Jackson looked at her scantily clad body. She hoped she looked as alluring as she was trying to be.

"I can't," he whispered, his gaze still glued to her form.

She grabbed his wrist and pulled him to her, forcing his body on top of her. "Stay. We'll have a sleepover!"

"Holly, I can't," he countered again, but made no move to leave.

"Stay." Holly let go of his wrists and her hands found their way to his firm, muscular shoulders. She reveled in his warm body pressing her down on the bed. His eyes focused on her and his breathing became shallow. She felt her own breathing grow ragged as his left hand settled in her hair. His other skimmed down her arm, sending shivers along her spine.

"This can't happen."

"Just stay and we can *talk*." She giggled, her voice sounding strange in her own ears. The room felt like it was moving, but the sensation of Jackson on her body grounded her firmly. She raised her hips against his and he groaned, his eyes closing.

"Holly, what are you doing to me?"

She smiled and moved against him again, feeling his firm manhood straining against his pants. "Stay with me." She sighed, her heart beating faster, heat pooling between her legs.

"Damn it," Jackson growled under his breath as

he slammed his full lips against hers.

Holly gasped at his sudden reaction but soon they fell in a rhythm of deep kisses, their bodies crushing against each other. His button-down shirt soon joined her dress on the floor, giving Holly full access to his taut torso. She skimmed her fingers down his back, feeling each muscle as he grinded against her. He palmed her breast, making a soft moan escape her lips.

Jackson buried his face in her neck as his hand explored her body—brushing her nipple through the lace of her bra with his thumb, running his fingers down her flat stomach, cupping her sex with his hand over her panties. It was all too much for Holly and she longed for more. She reached down and began to unbutton his pants.

Jackson pulled back from her to sit back on his heels, his breathing harsh. "Holly. No."

Holly pulled her hand back, her cheeks flushed, her body tingling with desire. "What's wrong?"

"You're drunk. I can't do this. You're my assistant." He stumbled over his words. "You've drank too much. I don't want to put you in this position."

She was dumbfounded. A moment ago, he'd been grabbing her breast and panting in her ear. "But-but…I want to."

"You're drunk. I can't do this."

"Okay." Holly sat up and pulled her knees to her chest, yanking the blanket up to her chin to hide her nakedness. Even though she was completely intoxicated, she was aware enough to be equally embarrassed by both her body and his rejection.

"I'm sorry," he said, stepping off her bed. He leaned down and gave her a soft kiss on the forehead. "Goodnight, Holly."

"Goodnight."

Then Jackson left her, closing the door behind him. Holly felt a tear slip down her cheek. She didn't understand what was wrong with her or why he didn't want to be with her. Then she felt the room spin. Her feelings could wait for morning. For now, she needed to sleep.

***

The next room over, Jackson sat on his bed, elbows on his knees and face in his hands. He was so close to having sex with Holly, the girl he'd hired to be his fiancée. She was right there in bed, wanting him, touching him, begging him to stay. But she was also drunk, far too drunk for him to justify sleeping with her. What if it was just the drink talking and she was not actually interested? Or worse, what if she was beginning to develop deeper feelings? He couldn't take that chance, no matter how badly he wanted her.

Their relationship was a business deal and he couldn't screw it up. He needed Holly, and the stability her presence offered, in order to become mayor. The business had been his birthright, the legacy his father created. But Jackson wanted to build his own legacy, one that made a difference, and he wouldn't let his own desires mess up his goals.

Chapter Six

The next morning, Holly awoke in her bedroom. Her shades were drawn, making the room dark, although according to the clock, it was already almost noon. Her head pounded thickly with each heartbeat. Moaning, she sat up and looked over at the nightstand for her phone. Beside her cell, which had been plugged in for her, she found a glass of water, two little pills, and a note. It read:

Holly,

Take these as soon as you wake up and try to eat something. You'll feel better. I'm sorry about last night. I'll see you after work. Call me if you need anything.

—Jackson

Holly groaned as the events of last night poured

back to her. In an alcohol-fueled haze, she'd thrown herself at her boss. She stripped in front of him and then pleaded with him to stay with her. But it hadn't mattered because he'd rejected her, just like she feared he would. She felt hot with embarrassment. She popped the Tylenol into her mouth and drowned it with a gulp of water. At least Jackson had already left for work hours ago.

The apartment was silent and the kitchen was empty. Mrs. Klein must've been out, and Holly was grateful that she could get something to eat without being questioned about her evening. She made some toast and scurried back to her room to get ready to go shopping. No matter how terrible she felt, it reminded her that she had agreed to do a job for Jackson, to look good on his arm, and she needed to uphold her end of the agreement.

***

"Hello, may I help you?" a matronly woman in a neon suit asked.

"Yes. I need a formal gown for an event tonight."

"Oh, the Annual New York Donors Ball?"

"Maybe? I'm not sure. My, um, fiancé just told me I needed a dress." She looked nervously at the thin mannequins draped in silk.

"Your fiancé?" The saleswoman looked at her closely. "You know, you look familiar."

"I don't see why. I've never shopped here before."

Recognition lit up the woman's face. "Oh my

goodness! You're the girl in the magazines. The ones who's dating Jackson Cantrell!"

Several other shoppers turned to look at her and Holly was suddenly glad she'd opted for a cute outfit of jeans and a silk top with some sturdy pumps instead of the sweatshirt and legging she almost wore. She lowered her voice to a whisper. "I'd really like some privacy while I shop, if that's all right. Can I just try on some dresses, please?"

"Oh, yes! Yes, of course!" She smiled, sneaking a glance at Holly's left hand. "You're really engaged to Jackson Cantrell?"

Holly blushed, slowly slipping her fingers behind her back. "Yes."

"You lucky, *lucky* thing!" She pulled Holly to the dressing rooms and placed her inside the largest one. "You stay right here. I'll go pull a few outfits for you and make sure no one disturbs you."

Holly slumped down in the dressing room's chair, dropping her purse on the floor. Now, the saleswoman knew who she was and that she was *engaged* to Jackson, not just dating him. She wondered how long it would take for the tabloids to pick up that little detail. No doubt it would soon be on the front cover of those celebrity magazines.

She debated calling her mother to let her in on the news before she heard about it through the tabloids. Her iPhone was heavy in her hand and her thumb hovered over her mom's contact info. But Holly stopped, remembering her non-disclosure agreement. She was about to call Jackson to ask for advice when the saleswoman swung the door open, a rolling rack full of gowns behind her. As she took in the rows of silk, feathers, sequins, and lace, Holly knew she was in over her head.

She hurriedly scrolled through the contacts in her phone before picking the name she needed the most at that moment. He answered after a single ring. "Daaaahling," Cosmo crooned. "I have been waiting."

***

A few minutes before eight, Jackson knocked lightly on Holly's bedroom door. He prayed there would be no lingering awkwardness from the night before. He had thought about the dejected look on her face all evening and couldn't bear the thought of making their agreement awkward. But when the door swung open, he was greeted with the overly Botoxed face of the stylist, Cosmo, who was shadowed by a thin woman carrying several bags.

"Ah, the prince is here for the princess," Cosmo simpered, tossing his long purple scarf over his shoulder. "Daaaahling, she is perfection."

Jackson swallowed a laughed and nodded somberly. "Thank you for your service. I assume this has been charged to my account?"

"But of course. I'll let myself out." Cosmo winked up at him before gliding down the hall.

"Jackson?" Holly's voice called from inside her walk-in closet.

"Yeah, it's me."

She appeared from within and Jackson's mouth grew dry as he took her in. Holly's deep green floor-length dress was strapless with a sweetheart neckline and a slit that ended high on her thigh. The fabric grazed her legs like liquid and showed just a hint of her gold pumps. Cosmo had given her an evening look with kohl-rimmed eyes and hair that fell in gentle waves over one shoulder.

"You look amazing, Holly. Seriously gorgeous." Jackson smiled softly at her, trying to ignore the strange lump in his throat.

"Thanks." She blushed, biting her lip in that innocently erotic way. "About last night, I—"

"Don't," Jackson said, placing his hand on her arm. "We don't need to talk about it. You made a delicious dinner and we both got carried away. Let's just have a nice night."

"Okay."

"And please cheer up. I got you a surprise."

Holly perked up, instantly back to her peppy self. "A surprise?"

"I can't let my fiancée go out without any diamonds."

She held up her hand, flashing her heavy jewel. "But the ring's right here."

Jackson reached into his jacket pocket, pulling out a red box that said *Cartier* on the rim. "That one doesn't count." He opened the box to display a set of teardrop shaped diamond earrings in a yellow gold setting. Jackson had canceled a lunch meeting to go shopping. He wanted to give her an apology gift, as well as a bonus for agreeing to come that night. As much as he didn't want to admit it, he actually enjoyed spoiling her. "I thought these would match whatever you were wearing. I'm glad I was right."

"Oh my gosh, Jackson. They're just too much!"

He frowned. "You don't like them?"

"I love them. They're so beautiful. They must have just been so expensive."

"Just take the earrings," he commanded, rolling his eyes. "What's the point of having all this money if I can't give my fiancée nice things?"

Holly popped out her modest diamond studs and put the new ones in, her fingers lingering on the new additions. "Thank you. I don't know what to say."

"You don't need to say anything. You look perfect," Jackson said, taking her left hand in his and raising it to his lips. He meant every word. "I couldn't imagine a more exquisite date."

Her cheeks pinked and she didn't answer, merely touching one of the diamonds. He thought he should say something else, but he didn't want to overstep the line that he basically leaped over the night before.

"Are you ready to go?" he asked, breaking away from his thoughts.

Holly nodded. "Lead the way," she told him, flashing a smile up at him as he led her out to the elevator without letting go of her hand.

"Adorable!" Mrs. Klein popped out from the kitchen, a camera in hand. "Let's just take a moment to get a picture of my favorite couple!"

"Mrs. Klein, his isn't prom," Jackson scolded.

The woman *harrumphed* and took the lens cap off the camera. "This place could use a personal touch, and what better way than to add some nice pictures of you two?"

"Fine." Jackson checked his watch. "Just a few, then we really have to go. Rick's waiting for us downstairs."

"Now, say cheese!" Mrs. Klein aimed her camera at the two of them as they posed for a picture.

***

Holly jittered with excitement when they reached the front of the building. She had never been inside a limo before and now she was taking one to a fancy event with a gorgeous billionaire, while wearing earrings as big as dimes on either side. She fought the urge to take out her cell phone and snap a few pictures. Obviously, Jackson was more than used to the finer things in life and Holly didn't want to look like a complete country bumpkin. But she did manage one when he wasn't looking. Her sister would never believe her otherwise.

Jackson opened the door for her and then slid in beside her on the seat. "Too ostentatious?"

"No. Maybe. I don't know." Holly pushed several buttons, opening a moon roof and turning the radio on and off.

"Haven't you ever been in a limo before?"

She shook her head, looking out the tinted window at the people on the sidewalks. She had often seen limousines in the city and always wondered what actor or model was riding inside. Now it was *her* people were curious about. "No. I've never had a reason to."

"Well, there's always a first time for everything.

But I must warn you about tonight."

"What is it?"

"This is a high-profile event," he told her, the MoMa rapidly coming into view. "There will be a lot of political powers here and big donors. The media will be out in full force. We're talking magazines and newspapers."

Holly bit her lip and looked at him anxiously, wishing she had called her mom earlier like she had planned. "Really?"

He gave her a small smile and took her hand in his, giving it a slight squeeze. "Yes. There are always paparazzi at these kinds of events. But don't be nervous. Everything's going to be all right."

Although his firm hold comforted her, it did little to calm the rapid beating of her heart. "People are starting to spot me all over the city. When I went to buy a dress, the saleswoman recognized me right away as your girlfriend, or fiancée, I guess. She saw the ring."

Jackson shrugged. "It was going to happen sooner or later. I just feel badly that you're stuck in the middle of all this. I'm very sorry that I keep dragging you into these things."

"For a successful businessman, you certainly don't think things through," she said, attempting to keep the mood light.

Holly sighed and looked past Jackson at the groups of people huddled outside the museum. As they pulled closer, she could see a red carpet spread out over the several yards to the front door and the flashes of cameras. She was about to walk a real red carpet and hundreds of people were going to take her picture. While many people dreamed of that, Holly was a little terrified. She wasn't used to walking in heels that high and a small part of her felt as if it was only a matter of time before she fell on her face. But when Jackson reached for her hand, her heart beat even faster. The nervousness dissipated, replaced by a feeling she wasn't quite ready to name.

"Ready?" he asked as they stopped at the edge of the carpet.

Holly nodded, plastering a smile on her face. "As ready as I'll ever be."

The driver opened the door for Jackson, who helped Holly out of the car. He gripped her hand firmly, securing her to his side as they made their first official public appearance together. The flashes blinded Holly, who fought to keep her smile looking natural and effortless. Although, she thought her face must have actually resembled one of those creepy porcelain dolls her grandmother collected.

She glanced up at Jackson. His face was relaxed, a slight smile playing on his lips. He looked down at her and gave her a small wink as he let go of her hand. Jackson quickly placed it on her lower back, allowing him to lead her through the crowd instead of pulling her behind him.

Holly relaxed as they made their way toward the entrance of the modern glass building. The end of their long entrance was almost in sight and so far, there were no giant disasters or even little slip-ups. At least she wouldn't be mortified if any of the pictures ended up in the magazines.

The photographers and reporters called Jackson's name for interview requests and pictures. But then they began to call for her. "Holly! Holly McIntyre! Miss McIntyre, over here! Holly, who are you wearing? Let's see the ring, Miss McIntyre!"

Holly felt her chest tighten. They knew her name *and* they knew she was engaged to Jackson. At least, they all believed she was. Now there would be no hiding her identity. Jackson wrapped his arm around her waist as they paused for pictures, leaning into her so there was no space between them.

"Are you all right?" Jackson whispered into her hair, sending a shiver through her body.

"I'm okay. You?"

"Well, I'm great. I have the best looking date here."

Holly knew he must have been joking, but her cheeks pinked all the same.

The reporters called out to Jackson, pushing against the rope barrier that kept them away from the red carpet. Some questioned his liberal political leanings while others asked if they'd set a date for the wedding. Holly tried to keep a polite smile on her face and let Jackson do all the talking.

He pulled her toward the door, his hand still firmly at her waist. When they entered the building, Holly thought that it didn't even look like a museum. The spacious lobby was filled with people in long gowns and tuxedos. Dozens of circular tables were spread about the room with large floral centerpieces made up of huge white peonies and neon purple orchids. The tables were set for dinner with crisp white settings and waiters walked around with dainty appetizers for them to snack on. The room was lit with purple and pink lights and a stage was set up on the far end of the lobby with a banner that said *'New York Donors Association'* on the front.

"Care for a drink?" Jackson asked her, a mischievous look in his icy blue eyes. "Maybe some red wine?"

Holly batted him playfully, trying to hide the sinking embarrassment that settled in her stomach. "Not funny."

"I disagree. You're perfectly charming when you're wasted."

Her cheeks burned. "I'm serious, Jackson. I don't know what came over me last night, I ju—"

"Learn to take a joke, McIntyre." He chuckled. "Now, what would you like to drink?"

"Surprise me. Something girly."

"All right. Wait for me here. I'll be right back." He gave her a final squeeze before detaching himself from her and making his way through the throngs of people.

Holly soon lost track of him in the crowd and stood there at the edge of the lobby watching the elegantly dressed men and women. She tried blending in with the crowd, but felt like she stood out because she was alone. Several people glanced up at her, recognizing her. She tried to look like she was comfortable, but she felt a bit out of place in this group of wealthy socialites. However, it was her job and she would perform it well.

"Holly McIntyre?" a voice inquired behind her.

Holly turned around to face a gorgeous brunette in a hot pink corseted gown. "Yes?"

"So you're the girl who locked down Jackson?" The woman's brown eyes narrowed and Holly remembered where she'd seen her before.

"And you're the girl in the Roberto Cavalli ads!" The model was even more glamorous in person. Holly fought the urge to ask her how she kept her skin so smooth.

"Obviously. So you're seriously getting married to Jackson?" Her question sounded more like an accusation.

Holly felt her heartbeat quicken and her eyes scanned the crowd for the man in question. "Why do you want to know?"

"I was just curious to see who snapped him up. I can't believe it's *you*." She sneered, looking her up and down.

Holly couldn't believe this stranger had the audacity to be so rude. Suddenly feeling brave, she held up her left hand, heavy with the engagement ring. "It would look that way now, wouldn't it?"

"How could he have chosen you? You're short, plain, and ridiculously average."

Holly tried putting on a mask of indifference. She wouldn't let the nasty woman know that her words cut her. "Okay, so why are you even talking to me?"

"Because this whole thing must be a joke. You're hardly his type," the woman purred, her eyes still lowered into dangerous slits.

"I'm apparently more of his type than you are since I'm the one with the ring. Now if you'll excuse it, it seems that my *fiancé* is coming back with my drink." Holly smiled sweetly at the model, who turned and scurried away before Jackson came into full view.

"Hey, Holly," Jackson said, looking around. "Were you just talking to someone?"

"Some crazy lady who apparently hates my guts."

He handed her a tall glass filled with ice and amber colored liquid. "Impossible. You're delightful."

"Not everyone thinks so," she mumbled, taking a sip of her beverage. It was a Long Island iced tea—her favorite. "How did you know to get me this?"

"It just seemed like something you'd like. Come meet some of the top suits around here." He held out his arm for Holly.

She allowed him to lead her around to a dozen different people. They all oozed money and the men leered at her while the women greeted her in a polite, yet aloof manner. Jackson shook hands, talked politics, and Holly was more than thrilled when dinner was announced and they took their seats at the table closest to the stage. Everything was fake—the smiles, the laughter, the nods of the men as they greeted each other. For a moment, she was almost glad her arrangement with Jackson was fake as well.

"Ready to run yet?" Jackson questioned, popping a cherry tomato from his salad into his mouth.

"No, it's just a little overwhelming," she said, looking around at the top-tier guests. "I mean, I'm sitting next to Nikki Hilton and there's a Kennedy at the next table."

"They always come to these sorts of things. You'll get used to them sooner or later. They're people, just like anyone else, just with better summer homes."

"And a winter home to ski, a place in Paris for the fashion season, and then their regular McMansion in New York," she grumbled.

Jackson laughed and Holly smiled, pleased she'd gotten the reaction out of him. His deep hearty laugh filled the room like oxygen. It was hard to ignore the effect he had on people. If nothing else, he'd make a persuasive mayor.

Holly fiddled with her napkin and peered about the room, still amazed at where she was. "After dinner can, we take a look around? I've always wanted to come here," she pleaded, itching to run free through the halls.

"Of course we can. When they serve dessert, there'll be some auction pieces for charity and then we'll have time to explore."

Holly smiled her first true smile of the evening, the embarrassment of the night before almost entirely forgotten.

***

As soon as Holly's tiramisu was served, a man stepped up to the podium on the stage. He introduced the charity as one that catered to all aspects of inner-city life. They funded school rehabilitations, women's shelters, and scholarships through their events. When he said that each place at the table cost a thousand dollars, Holly nearly choked on her dessert. She knew it was for a good cause, but it was almost staggering to think that these people had so much disposable income. When the auction began, Holly could have fainted.

"Our first piece on the auction block is a romantic private cruise for two to the Caribbean! Bidding begins at thirty thousand dollars," an announcer called.

"Thirty thousand!" someone shouted.

"Thirty-five!" another yelled.

The bidding rose until it was concluded at eighty-five thousand dollars. A racehorse sold for sixty thousand and a weekend in Paris went for one hundred thousand. Even Jackson got in on the action, buying a set of Super Bowl tickets for an obnoxious price that made Holly gasp. The rest of the bids sold for more than fifty thousand dollars. By the time the auction ended, the charity raised more than five million.

"Is it always like this?" Holly asked as the people around them started taking their checkbooks out.

"I suppose so. We do this maybe two times a year," he told her, draping his arm around the back of her chair.

"We?"

"Yes. I'm on the board. I help put these things together. Maybe you'd like to be on the planning committee?"

"The planning committee?"

Jackson began running his fingers lightly up and down her bare shoulder and the faint touch made her body hum. "Yes. I thought you were interested in being a big shot event planner?"

"Of course. I always wanted to do something like that on a larger scale. Doing weddings, and little parties, was kind of my thing in Michigan."

"What about high-end charity events like this?"

"It would be amazing," she declared, trying to downplay her excitement. "Could I really join the committee?"

"As far as everyone is concerned, you're the future Mrs. Cantrell and all doors are open to you." Jackson leaned toward her and murmured, his lips brushing against her ear. "Besides, who could ever say no to you?"

She felt her heart flip. "Stop being such a tease."

"I'm not being a tease, I'm being honest. *I* could never say no to you."

"Is that so?" Holly asked, keeping her eyes on the stage where someone was giving a speech. She had to pretend that her boss didn't affect her and that she had more power over how she was beginning to feel. It was time she tried to control him instead.

"Most definitely. Name anything in the world you want and you'll have it."

Holly tried to think of the most ridiculous thing she could. "An original Degas painting."

"Consider it done," he said firmly. "What else?"

She laughed. "A first edition signed copy of *The Hobbit*."

"A lover of the classics." He nodded. "You'll have it within the week. What's next on your wish list?"

"A private tour of the museum?" she asked hopefully, still dying to see the MoMA in its entirety.

"Too easy. I'll give you a private tour of every museum in the city. I'll shut every one of them down, just for you." He moved closer and Holly could feel his breath against her neck. "Name something else."

"I can't think of anything else. I guess I'm happy."

He stared at her for a second, barely moving. She thought he was going to kiss her. Their real first kiss. The first kiss that they deserved to share.

Holly's breath grew shallow as Jackson tightened his grip on her arm and began nuzzling his nose in her hair. His breath tickled her throat and when he whispered, "You smell amazing," Holly almost lost control.

"Jackson, you old dog." A deep voice interrupted their moment, and Jackson let go of her, much to Holly's disappointment.

Jackson turned toward the older man after a brief introduction. Holly took this chance to compose herself. There was no use getting all hot and bothered when there was no chance of actually getting close to Jackson. What would be the point anyway? A quick lay, and then the contract would be over. Holly was definitely not that kind of girl. She didn't do one night stands or sex without a commitment.

The memory of last night flooded back to her and she groaned inwardly. All right, she *usually* wasn't that kind of girl. She forced her breathing back to normal and ignored the wetness between her legs that betrayed her for the liar she was.

"I think I owe you a tour now. Still interested?" Jackson asked her once the potential voter had taken his leave.

Holly nodded and allowed him to take her hand. "Do you know your way around?"

"Fairly well," he told her, leading her to the elevator and up to the next floor. "I thought we'd look at a few exhibits, then end up back down at the sculpture garden."

"The sculpture garden?"

"Yes. It's one of my favorite spots. It's great at night." There was a twinkle in his eye and it excited Holly. Few men seemed genuinely excited to tour a museum, but Jackson looked as if he'd be there by himself, admiring art in all forms. At the moment, he was looking at her as if she was an exquisite French painting and she fought the glee it caused within her.

"Where are we going first then?" she managed to ask him, trying to draw her attention away from her beating heart.

"The contemporary gallery. It's the main spot here, so it'll have the basic pieces you need to see."

"Are we allowed to just wander around like this?" she asked, noticing how empty the halls were.

"When you've donated as much money as I have, you'll find the staff is willing to be more than agreeable."

Holly took Jackson's proffered arm as he led her through several galleries. She had never been to such a large museum and it was a novelty to be shown around by a sophisticated and handsome man like Jackson. Holly watched him out of the corner of her eye as he spoke animatedly. He took the time to explain each painting, sculpture, and installation to her. Although several of the pieces were bizarre, and Holly was fairly sure he made up facts about them, she listened eagerly anyway— *ohhhing* when appropriate and gasping on cue.

Hand in hand, they made their way through the indoor exhibits and then outside to see the sculpture garden. The excitement flowing through her made Holly feel as though she was soring on a cloud. Nothing could bring her down, especially if Jackson was beside her smelling like expensive cologne and fine scotch. It was almost more intoxicating than the Long Island iced tea she had earlier.

The sculpture garden was a large open space. It was made out of concrete and had an open roof that showed off the night sky. The multicolored lowlighting brought the several strange sculptures into focus. Lush trees and shrubbery surrounded a dark reflection pool and fountain. It seemed that by the time the pair made it back to the first level, the majority of the guests had left, making the low rush of the water the only sound they heard.

Holly felt guilty each time her heel clicked, creating a sharp sound that cut through the silence. "It's beautiful," she whispered, feeling the need to keep things quiet. There was something mysterious about this place and she wasn't quite ready to ruin the magic.

"Isn't it?" He turned her around and enclosed her suddenly in a tight embrace. Her back rubbed against the flat stone of a statue. "Thank you for coming with me tonight."

"Of course." Holly gradually placed her arms around his neck, bringing up her feelings of embarrassment of the night before when they were almost in this exact position. She looked down, afraid to meet his gaze. He must have been thinking about last night too, but she doubted it was in a positive light. At least, she doubted it until she felt Jackson move.

His hand slid up from her waist to the top of the slit in her dress, grazing the bare skin and giving Holly delicious goose bumps. The familiar feelings of lust in her chest heightened as he brought his face down to her level. She slowly pressed her body into his, giving him more access to her smooth thigh. For a brief moment, she wondered what it would be like to just rip her dress aside and let him push her up against one of the priceless statues, feeling only him and the smooth rock against her naked skin. The thought made her cheeks fill with heat, but didn't deter her from wanting it all the same.

"I mean it, Holly," Jackson whispered, his hand drifting dangerously close to her inner thigh. "You didn't have to agree to all this. You could have stayed in your quiet life just working as my assistant and living in your own apartment. Now I've forced you into the spotlight."

Holly's head spun, and it wasn't because of the drinks. "It's not that bad. Besides, you needed my help."

"So true. I really did—*do* need you."

"I need you too," she whispered without

122

thinking.

"Do you?" he asked, pushing up her dress slightly and touching her bare hip. "Do you need me?"

Holly felt her knees weaken as she pressed her breasts against his hard chest. "Yes." Her grip on him tightened as she leaned into his caresses, realizing just what she needed from Jackson.

"How badly do you need me, Holly?" His face was mere inches from her own and his hand explored her exposed skin. "Tell me."

When Jackson let his free hand cup her breast with a firm grip, Holly groaned, pulling him closer and begging him with her body to touch her more. The feeling of his strong hand through the smooth silk of her dress was driving her insane and she gripped his shoulders tightly, trying to anchor herself to reality. Before she could answer, the sound of people invading the garden broke them apart. A cluster of individuals began milling about the statues, forcing Holly to give up all hope of taking things further.

Jackson backed away from her, his lips tight. "I guess we're not the only ones who were hoping for a tour. Ready to go home?"

Holly tried to catch her breath while hiding her disappointment. She had never wanted a man so badly in her life.

***

As soon as the limo doors were shut behind them, Jackson closed the partition to the front of the limo, giving them much-needed privacy. He had basically rushed her out of the museum and into the waiting car, longing to get her alone. The way she looked up at him with her brilliant green eyes, her breasts thrusting against his chest and the feeling of her soft skin against his palm, made him want to pull the cloth aside and take her right there in the sculpture garden. When he realized she wasn't wearing any panties, it was almost too much.

He wasn't even sure he knew who this little minx was, but Jackson liked this new side of Holly. In fact, he liked all the sides he'd seen of her so far, and that was the problem. When he was around her, he let all of his rules go, giving it to the present.

"Did you have a good time tonight?" he asked, his fingers making lazy circles on her exposed thigh. Jackson watched as she bit her lip, leaning into him.

"I did," she breathed, opening her statuesque legs wider as his hand drifted inward.

He bent toward her and traced her collarbone, nipping at her neck. "I love you in this dress."

"I love you in your…clothes," she finished with a giggle. "I'm sorry, my brain isn't working right now."

Jackson skimmed her slit, watching as she gasped and clutched his arm. "Then just let go." He slipped a finger inside her. She was wet, willing, and completely melting in his hand.

When the limo halted to a stop before their apartment building, he placed a kiss on the curve of her neck, feeling her pulse race beneath his lips. He could smell the perfume in her hair—lavender and sage, mesmerizing him. He almost wanted to tell Rick to keep circling the block, but the car was dark and he hated the thought of taking her for the first time on the floor of a company vehicle.

"Here already?" She pouted prettily and pulled her dress back down over her legs.

"It seems so." His hands fumbled for the knob as he opened the car door into Rick's stomach in his haste to get home. "Sorry, Rick. You can have the rest of the weekend off."

Jackson pulled Holly through the lobby, ignoring the many people who stopped to look at the running pair. He hadn't felt so free in years. It was like a scene from a movie that Jackson had seen with one of his ex-girlfriends. But he'd never understood the need to be with someone like this. Sure, he'd wanted women before, but he'd never needed one. Until he'd hired one.

As soon as the private elevator doors were closed behind them, he pushed Holly against the wall, covering her mouth with his. He lifted her bare left up, wrapping it around his waist, before he slid his hand from knee to hip, enjoying the smooth, toned skin bursting to life under his touch.

When Jackson unlocked the front door, letting them inside the apartment, he was ready to forget everything and just be with Holly. He'd worry about the consequences later if he could just...

Ursula was sitting on the couch watching a movie. She turned toward them with a smile. "My *bébés*. How was your evening?"

Jackson shifted nervously, attempting to hide the bulge in his pants. "Mother, what are you doing here?"

"The people at the hotel, they do not listen. I say I need fresh pressed cappuccino, and then they give me regular coffee. I pay for perfection I expect perfection," Ursula said with a wave of her hand. "You cannot trust Americans to make a decent cappuccino."

"So you came here for a cappuccino?" Jackson asked dryly.

"No, no, no. I came to stay. I had my bags delivered and set up in one of the guest rooms. I thought you wouldn't mind," Ursula said.

"Of course not. Make yourself at home." Jackson smiled at his mother and took Holly's hand. "We're off to bed, we've had a long night."

"All right, *bonne nuit*. See you in the morning. I've made reservations for eleven." She turned back to the television, leaving Jackson and Holly to themselves.

Jackson ran his free hand through his hair and led Holly into his bedroom, all thoughts of sex forgotten with the sudden appearance of his mother. "You need to stay in here."

Holly reddened. "In here? With you? In your room?"

"It would look suspicious if we stayed in separate rooms," he told her, taking off his suit jacket and tie.

"Maybe she wouldn't notice. Maybe she would think we were being traditional."

"My mother isn't stupid. She assumes that if we live together, we sleep in the same bed." He smiled, trying to calm her. He hated the thought of making her uncomfortable. "Don't worry, though. My bed is large enough that you could completely sprawl out and not even graze me."

"But what about my pajamas and toothbrush?"

Jackson went into his walk-in closet and returned with a large white shirt. He debated giving a pair of his pajama pants, but came to the conclusion that they would be too big to stay on her slim hips. Or at least that's what he told himself. "You can wear this to bed tonight and there are new toothbrushes in the bathroom closet. I'll have Mrs. Klein move all of your things in here tomorrow while we're out."

He watched her as she went into the bathroom, caught up in the gentle sway of her silk-covered ass. Jackson grimaced, wishing he had just circled the goddamn block.

***

Holly took the shirt wordlessly and entered the spacious marble bathroom. She peeled off her dress and put the shirt on, wishing she had worn underwear. Now, she would be completely exposed in bed. Not that the lack of underthings had been something negative a few minutes ago.

Brushing the impure thought away, she tried to focus on getting to bed. Using some body wash she found in the shower, she took off her makeup. Then she brushed her teeth with a new toothbrush. Nervously, she looked at herself in the mirror, noting that the shirt thankfully came down low on her thighs and the v-neckline of the shirt was not low enough for any accidental slips to occur. She tried not to think about the fact that she was about to get into bed with her boss.

It was very risqué, no matter how innocent he made it sound, but even more ridiculous when she considered what almost just happened. Who decided it was more intimate to sleep *next* to a man than it was to sleep *with* a man? Things seemed pretty backward, but Holly couldn't shake her nerves all the same.

She took her engagement ring off and placed it on the marble top counter next to a flashy watch of Jackson's. She had tried to sleep with the ring on before, but her hair kept getting snagged in the golden setting.

Jackson knocked on the door. "You all right in there?"

"Yes, you can come in. I'm finished."

"No rush. You can go ahead and get into bed while I brush my teeth." He entered the bathroom dressed only in a pair of plaid pajama pants that hung low on his sculpted hips. Not half an hour ago, she'd felt those muscles under his tux and had wished for skin to skin contact. Now, she was almost embarrassed to look. Again, backward. She needed to get a grip.

Holly squeezed past him, holding the shirt down as she hurried to the bed. She slipped between the sheets and felt her body sink into the mattress. Jackson was right; his bed was huge, and as long as they stayed on their own sides of the bed, they would never touch. Although Holly was not exactly sure whether that was a good thing or not.

Being in Jackson's bed made her heart race. She

had been staying in his apartment, but this was the first time she was truly in his personal space. She was wearing his soft cotton shirt, sitting in his bed, smelling of his body wash, and still feeling flushed and aroused from their earlier interactions.

Holly scanned the room. Much like the rest of the house, it was furnished in a rich, classical style with a brocade comforter and fine art framed on the wall. The only pieces of personal memorabilia were an encased baseball on the mantle of his fireplace and a framed picture of him and his mother with the president. Everything else was uniformed and anonymous—completely unreadable, just like Jackson.

***

Jackson clutched the edges of the sink, trying to control his breathing. Holly was waiting for him in his bed and wearing nothing but one of his shirts. He imagined her long, smooth legs curled under his down comforter and her luscious hair spread over his pillows. The familiar stirring deep in his groin at the thought of Holly made him almost angry. She was the one woman he desired, but the one woman he should stay away from. She was his assistant and he'd hired her to *act* like his fiancée. He couldn't take advantage of her sweet innocence when he knew that he could never offer her true married life or his undivided attention like she deserved. This entire situation was built on a lie and he could not take the chance of growing too close to her. She was better than that.

Before he entered the bedroom, he splashed some ice-cold water on his face to cool his heated libido. It helped slightly, but he was still glad that a lamp on the nightstand only dimly lit the room now. Holly was sitting up against his headboard, biting her lip in that deliciously nervous way. He could tell she was anxious and he hated that he placed her in this compromising situation, but in a small way he was grateful that she was there.

"Do you need anything?" Jackson asked as he slipped in bed beside her. More than two feet separated them, but he could still feel the sharp electricity flowing through the covers. How in the hell was he going to sleep tonight?

"No, I'm fine." Her voice was soft and she glanced at him warily as she lay down and settled herself on the pillows.

"I told you my bed was large enough for the both of us," he teased. "You can pretend I'm not even here."

She turned on her side to face him and he could see the curve of her breast in the neckline of the shirt she wore. He fought the urge to reach out and touch her.

"I had a nice time tonight," she said, but it didn't break him out of his spell.

"Me too. You're not a bad date," he muttered, trying to move his gaze from her chest. He did not want to be a lecherous man, but he could not help himself. He slowly inched toward her, pretending he was merely adjusting his pillows.

"You're not too bad yourself, Mr. Cantrell." She brushed a stray lock of blonde hair behind her ear.

"Have you figured out what happens when this is done?"

"What do you mean?"

She bit her lip and paused before answering. "When all this pretending is over? I'm in the public eye now and I can't think of a clean way out."

Her question felt like a bucket of ice water had been poured over his head. He hadn't really thought about what would happen when she was no longer his fake fiancée. In fact, he hadn't really thought much about what would happen from one day to the next. And he certainly couldn't think about it with her so close to him now.

Instead of answering, Jackson took the time to study her face—the clean line of her nose, her bright green eyes that seemed illuminated in the sparse light. Holly looked better without makeup, fresher and cleaner. She was so much different than the girls he was used to, with their caked-on makeup and constant diets.

He hated waking up alone in bed as some model ran off to the gym, an actress rushed off to an early audition, or an heiress talked down to sweet Mrs. Klein about how she could only eat organic fruit. He liked knowing that Holly was going to be waking up with him every morning for the foreseeable future—at least in the same apartment, if not the same bed.

Even after a short week together, Jackson was already used to having her as a constant figure in his life. He wasn't sure he'd be able to let her go after the election, but he knew he had to. Jackson wasn't anywhere close to being ready to settle down and

Holly was the marrying kind—the bang her till she's sore kind, but still the marrying kind.

"I'm not sure," he replied honestly. "It isn't something that we can plan for anymore."

"Well, it's not like we can just live like this forever," Holly whispered. "We can't stop the truth from coming out."

Jackson sighed and turned on his back, facing the ceiling. "I know. I just don't know what to do. With the election, I let myself get talked into playing the part of a family man while, when it comes to my mother, I just wanted her to be happy and really support my political aspirations."

"Have you talked to her about this?"

"Yes, but she just won't listen. She ignores everything I say about it and completely blows me off. She grew up in a poor Romany Gypsy family and knows what true poverty is like. While politicians have money, it's the businessmen that make money. She never wants me to be without. But you being here has warmed her up to the idea of the company taking a backseat."

Holly sat up in bed, untangled herself from the bedding and leaned toward him on a raised elbow. Her blonde hair fell over her shoulders and her plump lips parted as she seemed to study him. "Us pretending to be engaged won't make her change her mind entirely, but I understand what you're trying to do. I'll even talk to her about it, if you want me to."

"You will?" Jackson sat up in bed. His sudden movement forced them to be so close to each other they could almost kiss.

"Of course. Don't you get it, Jackson? I just want to help you."

"How did I get so lucky to get such an amazing fiancée?" he asked her jokingly. He hated to end the night on a somber note, no matter how dark he was feeling on the inside.

"What can I say? I love a man in an expensive Italian suit with an American Express Black Card," she shot back with a grin.

Jackson laughed and placed a hand gently on the side of her face, cupping her soft cheek in his palm. "I mean it, Holly. I really couldn't do any of this without you. No one's ever tried to help me so much. Thank you."

Holly's cheeks turned a deep shade of crimson and Jackson could almost feel the heat radiating off her flawless skin. She averted her eyes before speaking. "Of course. What are personal assistants for?"

"Let's get some rest. It's the middle of the night and we need to be up early to wine and dine my mother."

She smiled and slid back under the covers. "You're right," she said with a delicate yawn. "Goodnight, Jackson."

"Goodnight, Holly," he whispered, turning out the light.

Chapter Seven

The next morning, Holly woke refreshed and fully rested. She could not remember sleeping so soundly in months. Jackson's bed was so comfortable and warm and...

Her eyes shot open and she realized exactly how she was sleeping. Her head was resting on his bare chest and one arm was draped over his torso. One of Jackson's arms clutched her tightly. His hand had slipped under her loose nightshirt and was touching the naked skin of her hip.

His rhythmic breathing was loud in her ear and she was frozen as she contemplated how she got herself into this position. As comfortable as it was, it was hardly appropriate.

Gingerly, Holly began edging herself toward the far side of the bed, away from Jackson. She hoped that she could free herself from his embrace before he awoke to find her wrapped around him in such a compromising position. However, he woke up before she had the chance to make her escape.

"Where are you going?" Jackson mumbled

sleepily. His eyes still closed, he reached toward her.

"Um...I..." She was at a loss for words. Her boss was officially awake and fully aware that they had been cuddling.

"Is it time to wake up?"

Holly glanced at the clock, noting that it was a little after nine in the morning. "Yes. I think we forgot to set an alarm."

"It's too early," he grumbled, turning on his stomach and forcing his face into the pillow. His usually tidy hair was messy and gave him a youthful look that Holly had never seen before. She longed to reach over and smooth down the wayward hair but couldn't bring herself to go through with it.

"Well, I'm going to go try and sneak into my room for a shower and a change of clothes before your mom gets up."

"Mrs. Klein moved your stuff. She put it all away in the bathroom and closet. I saw her doing it a few hours ago."

"Already?" Holly was shocked and her cheeks reddened. She was not usually a heavy sleeper, but for some reason she had slept through Mrs. Klein moving her entire wardrobe. And now the housekeeper knew they had spent the night together. Holly wasn't sure the thought bothered her as much as the fact the housekeeper believed they were already a loving couple. "All right then. I guess I'll start getting ready."

The hardwood floor was cold against Holly's feet as she rushed toward the bathroom for her shower. Although Jackson probably fell back asleep, she didn't want him catching a look at her bare legs. In the light of a new day, she was fully aware of how little she wore to bed the night before and the thought of it made her cheeks flush an even darker shade of crimson. At least now she'd have her own clothes to wear to bed so she wouldn't be in a position to take Jackson's things, even if she loved the faint smell of him that accompanied the shirt.

She looked around the bathroom to find that her things were already placed in the appropriate areas. Her toothbrush was in the toothbrush holder, her shampoos and soaps were in the shower, and her lotions and makeup were lined up neatly against the mirror. Her favorite silk robe was even hanging next to the shower. To anyone else, it would've looked as if they had been living together for weeks. Mrs. Klein was extremely thorough in her work and for that, Holly was grateful.

The hot water felt good against her back and washing her hair and body was like washing away all the questionable choices she made over the past few days. As much as she hated to admit it, Holly was falling for Jackson. He was kind, funny, generous, and made her entire body tingle at the smallest touch. However, he was still her boss and she knew this whole situation was merely so that Jackson could win the vote for mayor. It was temporary and she needed to remember that.

She had to learn how to distance herself from her work and focus on what her boss needed her to do without all the emotional strings that seemed to be multiplying. If not, then in a few weeks, she'd be left with a broken heart while he fought to change the world.

Holly blow-dried her hair and put on some natural makeup before donning her robe and making her way to the closet to look for something to wear. Jackson was out of bed and she thought she could hear him talking to his mother somewhere in the apartment. When she entered the closet, she found her clothes had been sorted by garment type and color. Mrs. Klein had even folded her panties neatly in one of the built-in drawers, Holly noted with wry amusement. She put on a pair of nude pumps, black skinny jeans, and a low-cut, billowy, white top that flattered her without showing all of her business. Almost forgetting, she ran into the bathroom to grab her engagement ring.

A very naked Jackson brushing his teeth greeted her as soon as she entered. She was frozen in place, her gaze glued to his naked form, both inappropriate and desirable. His muscular chest was well-defined and his legs were toned from many trips to the gyms and an active lifestyle. She dared not look at the place where his thighs met, but she would not get a chance, either. Jackson cleared his throat loudly.

"Enjoying the view, Miss McIntyre?" he jested, grabbing a towel off the rack and wrapping it around his waist.

"Oh my goodness, Jackson. I am so sorry." She threw her left arm over her eyes and blindly felt along the bathroom for the countertop. "I just came in here for the ring. I didn't know you were in here. I totally would have knocked."

"Relax, I was joking."

Holly's hand grazed something warm and she let out a small shriek of surprise.

"My arm," Jackson said helpfully, taking her hand and guiding it to the vanity.

She felt the metallic shape of the ring and she gripped it tightly. "Here it is," she said, her voice barely a squeak. "I'll be leaving now. I didn't see anything, I promise. Not that there wasn't anything to see. I mean, not see."

Jackson laughed openly, a deep and throaty sound that came from his gut. "Holly, you're ridiculous. Stop covering your eyes. You'll hurt yourself."

She uneasily lowered her arm and peeked over her sleeve. "I really am sorry about that. I didn't know you were even in here."

"Don't be sorry," he said, turning back to the counter and selecting a bottle of cologne. "Are you almost ready to go?"

Holly nodded and slid back out the door, shoving the ring on her finger. She closed the door behind her and paused a moment to catch her breath. It seemed that they were constantly putting each other in compromising positions. There was no way she could handle staying in the same room as him for the foreseeable future. Last night she could hardly sleep after their little conversation. She found him all too confusing. One moment, he made her feel so completely desirable in a way that only a man who is interested in a woman can. But in the next, he reminded her that she was an assistant and she was doing her job well.

As hard as it was to admit, she kind of did feel

like a hooker. One who was desired, used, and then left on the corner with some money and career advice. It was time she focused on getting the most out of this arrangement. She was ready to start exploring the event planning business. Being a lady of leisure just wasn't her style and she definitely didn't want to go shopping again.

***

"Holly, I need you to plan my party," Ursula announced over the rim of her Bloody Mary. They were sitting outside at a high-end café in the center of the city. The weather was perfectly crisp and the sharp smell of fall was in the air. Photographers had followed the trio to the restaurant, but were chased away by management and a few large bodyguards who seemed to always be hovering around them now.

Holly nearly choked on her bacon. "You want *me* to plan a party?" The party planning gods must have heard her plea.

"You want to be an event planner, no?" She raised an eyebrow.

"I do. I've just never planned anything large...just some things around town or at my parents' restaurant." Holly glanced at Jackson, who was suddenly very interested in a piece of toast. He had something to do with this, no doubt.

"Well, it will be small. A birthday party with only two hundred of my closest friends." Ursula waved her hand in the air dismissively.

"Two hundred people?" Holly paled. There was

no way she could handle that.

"More or less. I want it to be a costume party. Obviously, I'll be Marie Antoinette. I'll need themed cocktails and I prefer live music. DJs are not my thing."

Holly swallowed, trying to settle her racing mind. If she was going to be a big city event planner, she was going to need to get used to those kinds of monumental tasks. "Okay. I think I can handle that. Do you have a date in mind?" She hoped the woman wasn't about to suggest Halloween, as that was only a mere month away.

"The fifteenth."

"Of November?" Holly questioned. "December?"

"October." Ursula inspected her talon-like nails.

Holly gasped. "That's only two weeks away!" Ah, it would seem the gods had a sick sense of humor.

Ursula smiled and reached into her small Gucci clutch, removing a credit card. "You will be surprised how well people respond to money. Put whatever you need on this card. Also, invitations need to be sent out very soon. I'll make you a list."

Holly took the card, trying not to look as frightened as she felt. "Are you sure you want me to do this?"

The older woman looked at her like she did not understand the question. "You are to be my daughter-in-law. We need to trust each other, no? I trust you to plan my party."

Holly shifted guiltily in her seat, catching Jackson's eye. "I'll try my best, Ursula."

"*Merveilleux!*" Ursula clapped her hands. "The last party before my son becomes a married man. Have you picked a date? I long to see your wedding."

Holly bit her lip. "We haven't really decided yet. Maybe in the spring."

Ursula pursed her crimson lips thoughtfully. "Spring. That will not do."

"Why not?" Holly asked.

"I'll be *mort, ma chère.* Dead," she answered simply, taking a cigarette out of her clutch and lighting it at the table.

"Mother," Jackson said tightly, "stop being so dramatic. And don't smoke, you know what your doctor says."

Ursula waved his hand away. "I am a grown woman and if I want to spend my last days smoking like a chimney, you will let me."

"You're not even dying," he said in annoyed disbelief.

"For now," she said, tapping her cigarette into an ashtray.

"Jackson." Holly placed a hand on his arm. "Ursula, Jackson doesn't mean to tell you what to do. He's just worried about your health."

"We all die in the end. What difference will cigarettes make?" she asked, taking a drag.

Holly took a deep breath before continuing. "Jackson and I just got engaged and you and I just met. I feel like I haven't even gotten the chance to get to know you properly. Then there's a whole wedding to plan that we haven't even really talked about yet. It could be more than a year before we come close to walking down the aisle. Then what if Jackson and I have kids? I would want them to know their grandmother. Will you miss out on the wedding and grandchildren and holidays and birthdays because you end up with lung cancer?"

Ursula stared at her, her eyes wide, her lit cigarette dropping ash on the white tablecloth. Jackson gaped at her, as well. Holly bit her lip and waited for one of them to respond to her rant. When neither did, she began to think she'd severely overstepped some boundaries. She was honest, open, and seriously harsh in her outburst. But, as she had once lost an uncle to the ravages of lung cancer, she couldn't watch Ursula dig her own grave.

"Okay." Holly rose from her chair, grabbing her purse from the floor. "Now that I've firmly stuck my foot in my mouth, I think I'm going to go. You two enjoy your meal and I'm going to go…somewhere else."

She hurried from the restaurant and out onto the street. Ignoring the bodyguards and hailing a cab, she went back to Jackson's apartment to await him and the possible repercussions of her hasty actions.

***

"You're amazing." Jackson's voice startled an unaware Holly, and she glanced up in surprise. It was late at night by the time he came home and she was already planted in his bed wearing a pair of comfortable-looking shorts and a tank top.

"What?" She frowned slightly.

"I know you were put into a weird spot, watching us bicker about her smoking, but I really appreciate you speaking out. No one's ever stood up to my mother like that before."

Holly put down the magazine she was reading and brought her bare legs to her chest. "I—I'm sorry. I didn't mean to offend anyone."

"No, I'm glad you said what you did. That's what my mother needed to hear."

"Really?"

"Yes, you were perfect. I really think you made her consider her options. She put out the cigarette on the spot."

"She did?" Holly asked eagerly.

Jackson's heart tightened. "She did. And as I was leaving lunch, I realized I had some promises to fulfill to you."

Holly cocked her head, playing with the end of her braided hair. "What promise?"

"Wait here." He strode from the room to the hallway, bringing back a large, paper-covered object. Jackson had spent hours that afternoon calling his connections and outbidding all those in his way. "Come open it."

Grinning, Holly scrambled from bed. "You really didn't have to get me anything. You've already done so much."

"Just shut up and open the goddamn gift, Holly," he laughed, holding it upright for her to tear off the paper.

"Holy fuck." Holly gasped, covering her mouth with a hand. "You're joking."

"Nope. It's yours."

Holly inspected the canvas, tears welling in her eyes. "Jackson, is this a fucking real Degas?"

He nodded, satisfied in her response and amused by her sudden cursing. "It's called *Danseuses à la barre.* Do you like it?"

"I love it," she whispered, her voice cracking. "I can't believe you got me a real Degas."

"Believe it," he said, leaning it against the dresser. "I'm having someone pick it up tomorrow to have it framed. I'm just fulfilling my promise to you and thanking you for telling my mom to cut the shit."

"I just said what anyone would have." Holly wiped an emotional tear from her eye.

He pulled her closer so their faces were inches apart and his arm was firmly around her narrow waist. Jackson could smell the scent of her faint perfume and the heat emanating from her tiny body aroused him. "No, no one else would have had the balls to talk to her like you did. Hell, I don't think I even do."

Holly shook her head. "I didn't do anything. You're giving me too much credit. And you got me a fucking *Degas*, Jackson."

His lips curled into a smile. "I like that."

"Like what?"

"How you say my name."

***

Holly bit her lip, suddenly feeling the heat between them and the brush of his hand inching under the hem of her shirt. "It's just a name. You hear it all the time," she said, remembering her thoughts that morning about keeping everything professional. She was slowly coming to terms with the fact that it was never going to happen.

"But it's *you* saying my name."

Suddenly feeling braver than she really was, she whispered, "Jackson."

"Again." His fingers tightened on her back and his icy eyes smoldered.

"Jackson."

He groaned and pulled her to the bed so quickly, she almost didn't know how they got there. She lay on top of him, and between her legs she felt his manhood pulsing, making her body react. Her breasts were pressed against his firm chest while his hands roamed her body, stopping to cup her buttocks and pull her sex closer to his own. The feeling of him, hard against her, made her moan.

"Again," he ordered, his lips touching hers. He pulled the tie from her hair, letting her golden mane shower over both of them.

Holly paused a moment, taking in the view of the most powerful man in New York, who was now just beneath her. His eyes gleamed with lust and he jerked his hips up to grind against her in a rhythmic pattern. "Jackson."

"God, yes," he growled, crashing their mouths together.

For a brief second they moved together in perfect harmony before Jackson abruptly broke their kiss.

"What's wrong?" Holly asked, her brows creased with worry. One second he was groping her like a teenager and the next he looked like a trapped animal.

"We can't do this," he murmured, his hands still firmly planted on the bare skin of her back. "This wasn't supposed to happen."

"Seriously?" Holly could hardly believe he was rejecting her again. The past few interactions they had were lust fueled and steamy, but always cut short.

"It just feels so wrong. This was supposed to be professional."

She raised a brow, an odd anger filling her body. "Your cock between my legs doesn't *feel* professional."

He gaped at her, obviously surprised at Holly's sudden crassness. "I-I—"

"Shut up," she said, straddling him, her fingers working the buttons of his shirt. She almost expected him to stop her, but he seemed too shocked to move. Once his chest was fully exposed, she ordered him to take it off.

"Holly, what are we doing?" he asked, still complying with her direction.

"What we both want." Holly sounded braver than she felt as her lips collided with his. "We don't have to have sex just yet, but I need something. I can't have you lead me on like this."

"I'm not leading you on."

"At the dinner, you promised me anything I wanted."

"And I'll get you anything you want," he murmured as she ran her freshly manicured fingers down his chest.

"I want you to stop whining. And I want you to

stop leading me on."

"That's not my intention."

"Then prove it," she said, pulling her tank top over her head and throwing it to the floor.

His hands grabbed on to her lace-covered breasts and she came down hard on his manhood, equally enjoying the sensation. She dragged her tongue down his muscular torso, feeling him tense up in arousal. Holly fumbled with the buttons on his slacks but quickly freed his member from his pants and took him into her mouth.

Jackson moaned as she licked up the length of his shaft, whispering her name. "God, Holly, I can't take it. You're too good."

She smiled, glad she was finally fulfilling what they both needed. She watched him convulse with each flick of her tongue, his eyes closed in ecstasy as his fingers tangled in her hair. When he finally rumbled in climax, she took it gratefully, her mouth firmly about his cock.

As soon as he finished, he dragged her upward, slamming her against the bed, settling himself between her thighs. Holly panted in anticipation as he slipped her panties down her legs and threw them to the floor. With a mischievous grin, his face drifted downward, settling on her sex. No one had ever done *that* to her and she blushed at the thought of him being so intimately acquainted with her. But she was the one who'd pushed forward and it was too late to back out now.

Her toes curled as she felt a wave of orgasm wash over her. She clutched the bedspread and cried out, catching a glimpse of an accomplished looking

Jackson between her knees.

"Was that enough for you?" he asked smartly, crawling up to the top of the bed.

"That was so incredible," she breathed. Holly couldn't feel her legs and merely closed her eyes, enjoying the relaxing moment of mutual release.

He lay down next to her, an arm draped over her waist. "You're just full of surprises, Holly McIntyre.

"A surprise for a surprise," she replied with a grin. And not even for a second did she regret it.

Chapter Eight

"Oh my God. There's no way I'll be able to pull this off," Holly groaned, dropping into one of the chairs in Jackson's office.

He sat behind his desk, clicking away at his keyboard. "Yes, you can. Just throw a party. It's no big deal."

"No big deal?" Her green eyes widened. "Jackson, I've never held an event this size before. I don't know what vendors to use or what your mother even likes. What if I order crab cakes and she's allergic to shellfish?"

"You're really thinking too far into this."

"I don't think so. What if I mess it up?"

"You won't. I have faith in you. Just get the best of everything and go big. My mother is a flashy woman. When you think something is too shiny or ostentatious, get the bigger size."

"I know, but I just don't want to disappoint her."

Jackson stopped working at his computer and circled the desk until he knelt beside her chair. "Holly, look at me. You can do this. You're

149

creative. You won't disappoint her, I know you won't."

"You really think I can pull this off?" she asked with a small smile.

"Of course. You're a people pleaser." His lip curled into a smirk and Holly playfully kicked him away with the toe of her Jimmy Choo.

"Don't you have important businessman stuff to do?"

He stood, looking at his watch. "I suppose so. How about you use my office for a few hours to start the planning. I have to go to a few meetings, but I can swing by after to get you for dinner."

"Sounds good."

"Rick's in the lobby, so just holler if you need anything." He brushed a hand against her cheek and placed a chaste kiss on the top of her head.

"I'm on the top floor behind, like, four secure doors. I'm sure I'll be fine," she said to his retreating form.

Holly slipped behind the large desk and took an inventory of Jackson's workspace. Most of the drawers were empty aside from a few pens and a pad of blank paper. A sleek laptop sat on the desk next to a phone. There weren't any personal pictures, knickknacks, or even a calendar. She assumed she would have been the keeper of his calendar, if she still worked as his assistant, and briefly wondered who was in charge of his schedule now. The tiny office looked empty and just as she'd left it.

From inside her purse, Holly retrieved the long guest list Ursula had left her. It was full of New

York City socialites, models, actors, business tycoons, and fashion designers. It would be a star-studded event, to be sure. That fact alone made Holly break into a cold sweat when she envisioned planning this party. If it didn't go well, no one else in New York, or probably the rest of the world, would ever dream of hiring her to plan an event. If she did pull it off, then she would surely have a waiting list for all the parties she would have to plan in the future.

Holly turned on Jackson's computer and pulled up the Internet in order to look at potential venues. Google was already open when she signed in. Filled with a sudden burst of curiosity, she typed Jackson's name in the search bar. It was almost astonishing to her that she had never looked him up before. Hundreds of results popped up that were mostly selections from celebrity blogs, company mentions in the paper, and philanthropic event newsletters.

However, there were also dozens of pictures showing Jackson with his arm draped around some gorgeous starlet with sky-high legs and bedroom eyes. Seemingly unable to control herself, Holly clicked through the pictures, mentally noting the differences between her and the girls he actually dated. While they were thin, she was curvy. Their exotically dark features were also in severe contrast to her own light ones.

It was easy for Holly to see why he couldn't think of sleeping with her. She was short, plain, and far less alluring than those famous starlets. Slightly queasy, she turned the computer off. She no longer felt like party planning. She pulled her cellphone from her bag and dialed Amber's number. The potential for some lighthearted female companionship was looking pretty good to Holly at that particular moment. Besides, Amber was a nice girl, and she could tell they had the potential to be great friends.

"Hey, girl, what's up?" Amber said, her voice cheery.

"Nothing much. I wanted to know when you had time to get together. I'm sure your hours as a nurse can get a little crazy sometimes."

"And I know your hours as a media darling are equally demanding." She giggled. "I'm actually off the next two days."

"Really? Think we can go get coffee or something? I'm supposed to be planning Ursula's birthday party, but I don't even know where to start."

"You're planning Ursula Gaspar-Cantrell's party? No way."

"You know her?"

"You seriously don't get out much, do you? She's only one of the most fabulous women ever! The Lifetime Channel even made a biographical movie about her life."

Holly was taken aback. There was obviously a lot she didn't know about Ursula. "Yeah, I guess I never followed pop culture in Michigan."

"Now's a good time to start. When's the party? Where is it? Are you getting something crazy like fireworks? That would be awesome."

"No clue. I have to have it together for October

fifteenth."

Amber gasped. "That's two weeks away!"

"I know. I don't even have anything done. I need to find a venue first."

"Then that's what we're doing today."

"I couldn't drag you around to look at venues all day," Holly said, spinning in the office chair to look out the floor-to-ceiling windows.

"Holly, I want to. Who knows when I'll ever get a chance to see how the other half lives?"

"You'd really come with me?"

"Obviously. Where can I meet you?"

"I'll have Rick come pick you up. He'll take us wherever we want to go."

"Ooh, a driver? How fancy. See you in a bit," she said, squealing with delight before hanging up.

Holly picked up her phone and told Rick about her plans. Hopefully, the party wouldn't be a *total* disaster.

***

"Girl, I wish your man had a brother, a cousin, or even a nephew. I'm not picky." Amber laughed as they sat in a small bakery by Cantrell International. She'd been an invaluable resource for party planning. Since she had lived in the city for so long, she knew the top spots for holding events. She'd never been to one of them, but she followed the media enough that sometimes she felt like she'd once been an honored guest.

"I couldn't have done this without you," Holly told her, taking a bite of a cake sample.

153

"Anytime you need me to eat cake on your mother-in-law's dime, I'm all for it!"

"May I get you Mademoiselles anything else? More coffee?" the baker asked, holding a steaming pot of French press. Everything in the bakery was French—the cappuccino, the croissants, and the portly baker.

"Please." Amber held out her cup with a grin. "By the way, this lemon poppy seed cake is to die for."

"I agree." Holly pulled out the small notebook she had brought with her, making notes on her makeshift spreadsheet. "I'll need a tiered cake in the lemon for two hundred."

"What about cupcakes?" Amber asked.

Holly paused. "You don't think the cake will be enough?"

"Girl, rich people love miniature stuff," Amber said in a serious manner.

The baker nodded enthusiastically. "*Oui!* Our cupcakes are some of the finest in the city. Our best sellers."

"Cupcakes," Amber ordered, pointing at her cake samples.

"Which ones, Mademoiselle?" The baker asked, holding a pen up to his clipboard.

"Cupcakes," Amber said again, gesturing to her entire plate.

The baker smiled. "Of course, Mademoiselle."

"Your new mama should have parties more often." Amber laughed as the baker retreated to tally the cost.

"And you should plan parties. Seriously, you

know all the hot spots people like. I would've had no idea what to do without you."

Amber waved a hand. "No biggie. This is way more fun than sitting around at home watching television."

Holly paused, thinking about her budding event planning business. "Amber, what if we could do this kind of stuff all the time?"

"Eat cake?"

"Get *paid* to eat cake."

Amber frowned. "Like a weird fetish kind of thing?"

"Oh, goodness, no." Holly gasped. "I mean event planning. I have the connections and you have the knowhow. We could do this together."

"As a job?"

"Yes! You were saying earlier that you were tired of your terrible hours at the hospital. If we did this together, we could make our own hours. Ursula said she had a whole list of friends who want to throw parties." Holly's mind raced as she spoke.

Amber tapped at her chin, feigning several moments of indecision before answering. "Hell, yes! Now, we're going to need some cocktails to go with this cake."

***

Holly stood at the kitchen counter, cutting vegetables with a practiced hand, when she heard the front door open and close. The clock showed it was barely four in the afternoon and she wondered why Jackson would be home from work so early.

"Holly? Are you home?" he called from the entryway.

She wiped her hand on her apron and left the kitchen. "Hey, is everything okay?"

He looked her up and down, appraising her. "Nice apron."

Holly narrowed her eyes. "When your jeans are two hundred dollars a pair, you take the proper precautions." She noticed he had a stack of magazines tucked under his arm. "Doing some light reading?"

"Technically, my manager, Denny, was doing some light reading." He loosened his tie as he spoke. "He pointed out how weird it looks that you basically appeared out of thin air."

"Because I did."

"But no one needs to know that. Look, Denny had an idea and I think we should go for it."

Holly could tell that Jackson was dancing around the topic. "Spit it out."

"Pictures," he said enthusiastically, dropping the magazines on a low side table. "We take a bunch of pictures. We'll have different outfits, themes, locations—all spanning the length of our relationship. Even my mother is wondering why she never saw anything about the engagement."

"How the hell do you expect we'd be able to take over Times Square without anyone noticing?"

"We don't have to. I found a guy who can edit some pictures with us in front of a green screen." He grinned, obviously thrilled with his plan. "We can have a Times Square proposal, escapades to the Cape, horseback riding through the country, and ski trips. It'll really give our romance story some heft with the public."

Holly crossed her arms. She could see the merit in his idea, but still hated the part about adding more proof to their lies. But she could also see how suspicious it was that she'd just shown up, rock on her hand, the moment Jackson's numbers hit their all-time low.

"All right, when is this happening?" she asked, turning back to the kitchen.

He followed her at a short distance. "Tomorrow. I told him it was an emergency."

"Did he sign a non-disclosure agreement?"

Jackson let out a short laugh. "Thinking like a true woman of the public."

"Well, did he?"

"Yes, and so did his photography assistant and the wardrobe woman who will dress us tomorrow."

"Can I call Cosmo?"

Jackson shrugged. "Whatever you need."

Holly picked up her chopping knife and turned back to the red peppers. Jackson came up behind her and snatched a piece, popping it into his mouth. "Hey, stop being a food thief."

Jackson pressed his lips to the skin of her shoulder, left bare by her tank top. "What are you cooking?"

"I was prepping for stir-fry tonight, but it looks like you might be hungry now."

"Oh, I'm hungry, all right." He nipped at her neck and wrapped a hand around her middle.

Holly felt her face flush, recalling their last romp in the sheets. "You're terrible."

"Terribly hungry."

She turned, knife in hand. "Then sit down and let me cook in peace."

***

Holly shifted from one foot to the other as the photographer, a serious-looking man named Hank, picked at Jackson's clothes and hair. They had been standing under the hot lights for quite some time and Holly's patience was wearing thin.

"We're supposed to look natural, right? I don't think all this poking and prodding is necessary," Jackson grumbled. "I'm sweating balls under this ski suit."

"I'm making you look natural," Hank said, tilting Jackson's head a quarter inch to the left.

Holly groaned, breaking out from the position the photographer placed her in. "I'm sorry, but I'm literally going to have a heatstroke. Jackson, I know this is your show, but you need to speed things along before I die. I've sat through fake sailing, a fake picnic, and a fake stroll through the French Quarter of New Orleans. I refuse to drop dead while fake skiing."

The photographer frowned. "Art takes time."

"I'm about to pull out my cellphone, take some selfies, and call it a day." Holly mumbled, fanning herself with a hand.

"No!" Cosmo gasped. He'd been watching the proceedings from behind the photographer ever since he'd finished Holly's hair and makeup hours before. "No one takes *selfies* after having their heads done by Cosmo!"

Jackson grinned. "I'm on her side. It's great you want it to be perfect, but we're dying over here."

The man let out a small breath through his teeth. "Fine, we do things your way."

"Finally." Holly zipped up her powder blue jacket and adjusted a pair of fluffy white earmuffs.

A few short shots and an outfit change later, they stood before the green screen for their proposal picture. Jackson had on a plain white button-down shirt and jeans while Holly wore a muted pink sundress. They were about to start when Cosmo ran onto the set, waving his arms.

"Wait! We must cleanse her face and replace it with an earthy smokey eye!" he shrieked. Hastily, he grabbed Holly's hand and pulled her into her dressing room, where his mass supply of makeup was spread over the countertop.

She fell into the seat and took a swig from her water bottle. "It's so much cooler in here."

"Oh, yes, the sparks are certainly flying on set!" Cosmo sang as he wiped off her makeup.

"Sparks?"

Cosmo nodded, dabbing fresh foundation on her chin with a little pink sponge. "The electricity between you two flows. No matter what you have on paper, you cannot hide it. Cosmo knows this to be true."

"What are you talking about?" Holly wasn't sure, but she had the feeling Cosmo had more than a faint idea about her and Jackson's arrangement.

"Turn your face to the left." He swiped against her cheek with a brush. "Cosmo sees everything, knows everything, is told everything…even things that are never said."

"How mysterious."

"Face right." Another dab of makeup. "It is not mysterious. You wouldn't be the first couple to begin in this way, with rules on paper and little agreements in writing."

Holly opened her mouth to respond, but he shushed her.

"Yes, Cosmo knows your secret, but Cosmo is a secret keeper. Can you keep a secret?"

Holly nodded.

"Cosmo was not always Cosmo," he began as he picked up a pallet of makeup. "Cosmo was once…*George*." He cringed and sputtered dramatically as if the words were something slimy he needed to get out. "George from *New Jersey*."

She stifled a giggle. "*That's* your big secret?"

"Close your eyes," he instructed, back to business with a small brush for eye shadow in his hand. "In a way, yes. George from New Jersey was quiet and shy and everything Cosmo is not. When George came to New York City, he went from a little grub to a beautiful monarch butterfly. What started as a lie, turned into Cosmo. You see?"

"I think?" She tried to focus on his words, but her mind kept drifting to thoughts of Cosmo as a caterpillar.

"What Cosmo tells you is that Cosmo started as a lie. It started as a persona that was fake in every way. But after years and years of living as Cosmo, George became Cosmo and Cosmo he will stay, happily. You started as Holly from Michigan, but

160

now you are living as Holly from New York City. It begins as lie and turns into truth. If it is *your* truth, then it is no longer a lie."

Holly opened her eyes and looked up into Cosmo's tanned face. "So you're telling me that I'm not really lying if this is where I want to be?"

Cosmo tapped the tip of her nose with the end of a makeup brush. "Yes, yes! You can be born a George and live as a Cosmo. And who wouldn't want that!"

Holly pondered his words as he finished up her final makeup. For such a strange character, he was the wise mentor she never had and didn't know she needed. And while he had an odd way of explaining it, Holly understood what Cosmo meant by saying her lie could become her truth. If only she could keep her head above water long enough to paddle through.

***

Hank handed Jackson a ring box, already stashed with Holly's diamond. "Now, look like you're in love."

Holly's lips twitched as she tried to control a fit of giggles that Jackson thought was about to burst. "I feel so stupid," Holly whispered, her grin looking almost unnatural.

"Relax," Hank ordered. "You're having a nice day, you just got brunch, you two love each other."

"Yeah, relax." Jackson pulled Holly close in an intimate-looking embrace.

"Better, better. Yes, good." Hank's flash

momentarily blinded Jackson as the photographer took pictures in rapid succession. "Now, Jackson, get down on your knee. Holly, you look shocked."

"Oh, my!" Holly's mouth snapped open and her hand flew to her cheek.

Jackson snorted. "Drama queen."

Hank's face was hidden by his camera. "Now, Holly, tears would be nice. Jackson, swoop her up. I want kissing, crying, then you put the ring on her finger. Be organic, excited. Really sell it."

Jackson shrugged and stood up, swooping Holly up and swinging her around, planting his lips on hers. With her breasts pressed to his chest and her perfume swarming around his head, he felt himself getting carried away. He opened her mouth with his tongue as Holly's fingers groped his hair. She ran her hands down to his neck and moaned into his lips. He felt himself harden and—

"Ahem." Hank stood, tapping his foot. "If this is going to be *that* kind of shoot, you're going to need to pay me extra."

Jackson placed Holly on her feet, liking how deeply she blushed. "No, sorry, Hank. I think we're done here."

"Wait," Holly said. "We haven't done anything campaign themed."

"Campaign themed?" Jackson thought a moment. While they had something fun for the gossip rags and his mother, they hadn't done anything official looking. Holly was always full of surprises, usually good ones. "Yeah, we should do some nice portraits."

Moments later, Jackson sat before a plain gray

background, waiting for Holly. When she stepped out of the dressing room, she was clad in a blood red shift dress, her hair blown out and makeup redone by Cosmo's careful hand. He couldn't help but grin as she stood there, looking every bit like a high society woman. The many ways she could transform herself was impressive.

This last shoot was shorter, more serious, with both taking turns at the seat while the other stood stoically by their side. Jackson thought it would be much more amusing to continue with their fake proposal. But each time Holly moved, innately in tune with his every motion, Jackson felt that maybe he'd found a true partner. Suddenly, when he looked at her, the awe in his eyes wasn't faked.

Chapter Nine

"Busy tonight?" Jackson asked as Holly tapped away on his laptop. She had been frozen in the same spot since he returned from work, poring over RSVPs and finalizing the menu.

"By busy do you mean trying to please all of New York society?' She spoke without looking up from the screen. "Then, yes, maybe just a little."

He watched her work, dressed in a Juicy Couture sweat suit with her hair in a ponytail. Her bright-red nails flew over the keys as she typed and every so often, she read something aloud and scrunched up her nose delicately.

"Do you want to take a little break?" Jackson sat on the bed beside her. "We can go grab some dinner."

"I'm starving." Holly paused, looking at the screen. "I guess I can finish this later." She closed the laptop and stretched a bit, like a cat. "What are you in the mood for?"

"Well, I actually made us some reservations."

"Oh, where?"

"Just a little place owned by a friend." He grinned, hoping she would be impressed with his choice. "Go get yourself pretty so we can go."

She frowned, a small pout on her lips. "You mean to tell me that my messy hair and sweatpants aren't dinner-worthy?"

"If you want to leave now, just as you are, then go ahead and put on some shoes." He smiled, thinking that she *did* look fine.

Holly hopped off the bed and went into their shared closet. "What should I wear?"

"Anything you'd like. You always look amazing," he answered, watching her shadow through the open closet door. Jackson heard the sounds of her clothes dropping to the ground and resisted the urge to go to her.

The past three days at the office, all he'd thought about was the feeling of her lips on his body and the sounds she made when she came. Although they hadn't touched more than a passing caress or light kiss, it wasn't for lack of trying. His mother lurked around every corner.

From the moment Jackson came home from work, until the early hours of the morning, his mother was dictating notes to Holly, both of them curled up on the living room couch with seating arrangements and menus. Tonight, Jackson had ensured she was kept busy getting her tickets to a prime Broadway show. He needed Holly all to himself.

"I just have to throw on some makeup and brush my hair." Holly stepped out of the closet in a fitted black dress, a thin white belt around her narrow waist. A pair of black heels were hooked on her crooked fingers.

Jackson nodded wordlessly, his gaze focused on her shapely form. He loved watching her do these mundane tasks. She did everything with such thoughtful precision. As time passed, he found it harder to keep from falling for the girl from small town Michigan, especially as he watched her transform into the society woman before him.

**

"So, what's this place?" Holly asked as Rick dropped them off in front of a brick building.

"Only one of the best restaurants in the city," Jackson said, placing his palm on her lower back.

Haute was intimate, candlelit, and exclusive. They were shown to a small table along the floor-length window that overlooked the city. He watched as Holly looked around at the white linen tabletops. If it was even possible, she looked even better lit by the backdrop of the city on her delicate features.

"What are you getting?" Holly asked, her bright green eyes scanning the menu. She bit her lip and brought her gaze to his, giving him a small smile.

At that moment, Jackson couldn't care less what he ate. "How about you pick for the both of us?" He closed his menu as a waiter filled their water glasses.

Holly frowned and paused before folding the menu. "I can't do it."

"Not feeling it?" Jackson asked, his lips

twitching in amusement. Maybe he could get her home early, after all.

"Is it obvious?"

"Maybe just a little."

Holly giggled. "I'm sorry, *squid eggs*?"

Jackson let out a laugh. "You're right, it is *shit*. I just wanted to treat you somewhere nice."

"Can we bail and get some real food, please?" Holly asked, her gaze nervously aimed at their waiter who was on his way over. "Or would that be super rude?"

"Let's go." He stood and held out his hand to her. He nodded at the waiter and slipped him a tip before taking her down the flight of stairs and out to the busy street below.

"Now what?" Holly looked around at the blank apartment buildings on either side. "We didn't call Rick and tell him to come get us."

"Just tell me where you want to eat. SoHo? Drive down to Jersey? Jet up to Maine and get some real lobsters?"

"The funny thing is I know you're not joking about flying to Maine just for dinner."

"I never joke about seafood," Jackson said, his brows furrowed in mock seriousness. He thought back to his musings about taking her to Barbados. He'd have to cancel some meetings, set up a villa, and move some things around, but it would be worth it to get her all to himself and scantily clad, due to the tropical climate. "Holly, how about we really get out of here?" he asked, almost without thinking of the repercussions.

"You want me to call for Rick?" She reached

into her handbag and pulled out her phone.

"I mean *really* get out of here, just the two of us." Jackson took the phone from her and slipped it back into her bag. "Let's go away. I want to take you on vacation."

Holly looked up at him from under her dark lashes. "A vacation? But why, when there's so much to do here?"

"Can you lay on the beach in New York City? Can you go snorkeling? Zip-lining?"

"No…"

He pulled Holly to him and skimmed her sides with his fingers, thinking of all the things he wanted to do to her. "Holly, I want to take you to Barbados."

***

"Barbados?" Her jaw dropped. She'd only been to three states in the U.S., and the Canadian side of Niagara Falls. She was hardly a world traveler.

"Yes. You'll love it! We'll leave tonight." With his arm still around her, he hailed a cab and stuffed her inside before pulling out his own cell. "Smyth, it's Cantrell. Ready the jet for forty minutes. I'm going to Barbados." He hung up the phone and redialed. "Mrs. Klein, pack bags for me and Holly for three days in a tropical climate, please." One last call: "Rick, Mrs. Klein has luggage for me. Pick them up and bring them to my hangar at JFK."

Holly's mind spun with how quickly it happened. There was only one problem. "Um, Jackson, there's an issue with this whole vacation idea."

He looked at her curiously. "We have a plane, luggage, and we're going to have accommodations by the time we get there. It's not as if you have to ask your boss for time off."

"I don't have a passport." She cursed herself for never seeing the point in getting that stupid little booklet.

"So?" he asked, turning back to his phone and tapping away.

"So, what about customs? I can't get into another country without a passport."

Jackson sighed and put down his cell. "Holly, stop worrying so much. We're flying private into an American-owned resort. I'm taking care of everything." He took her hand and pressed his lips to her knuckles as the airport came into view. "Not to be elitist, but certain rules don't apply to us."

"But what about the party?"

"We'll only be gone a few days. Things won't fall apart without you."

Holly jittered a bit as they neared the front of the terminal. Jackson paid the taxi and waved a car forward. It was Rick with their bags. Holly thought she'd never stop being surprised at how smoothly money made things go. She was still thinking about the speed with which the entire trip had been planned when Jackson helped her into the back of the town car and they drove around the side of the terminal to a small gate before the tarmac. A security guard waved them through almost immediately and Rick pulled the car right up to an idling jet.

"This is crazy. I've never even been on an airplane before," she whispered as Jackson walked her to the jet where a pair of pilots stood before a set of steps. She felt like an actress and couldn't control the bubble of glee rising in her chest.

"Private's the only way to fly." Jackson grinned and greeted the pilots, who followed them up and into the plane with their bags.

Holly looked around at the interior of the personal plane. To her right was the cockpit, but to the left was a jet interior right out of a reality television show. To one side was a pristine cream-colored couch and to the left was a pair of plush seats on either side of an elegant wooden table. A flat screen was mounted on one corner above a bar and a small kitchen flanked a door.

"Impressed?" he asked as Rick entered the plane with two paper bags.

"Very." Holly sat down, almost giddy with excitement.

Rick wished them both a good flight before departing. Jackson held out one of the bags to her as the pilot closed up the plane and prepared for takeoff. She peeked inside to find a cheeseburger and fries.

"Ugh, I think I love you." She moaned as she pulled out some fries. A good, old-fashioned burger beat out fancy squid eggs any day of the week. She gratefully took a bite.

Jackson crossed to the fridge and pulled out two sodas. "Happy?"

"Jackson, this is amazing. Seriously, no one would ever believe this. I'm in a private jet eating burgers on my way to a vacation with a billionaire. So crazy." She could hardly believe it herself.

"Good evening, Mr. Cantrell and Ms. McIntyre," the pilot said over the intercom. "We have been given clearance to taxi onto the runway. So, if you could take your seats and fasten your seatbelts, we can be on our way to sunny Barbados."

Holly smiled across the table at Jackson as the plane took off, on to their new adventure.

Chapter Ten

Holly felt as if she had just gotten to sleep when the pilot jarred her awake.

"Good, morning, Mr. Cantrell and Ms. McIntyre. It is five-fifteen in the morning and it's a balmy eighty-seven degrees and partly cloudy," the pilot announced in a cheerful voice. "If you could please take your seats, we'll be preparing to land shortly."

She rolled over in the private jet's king-sized bed, groping for Jackson. When she felt nothing more than pillows, she opened her eyes. The door to the main plane was open and she could see him in the kitchenette and smell the scent of fresh coffee.

Holly slid out of bed and opened the single dresser to pull out the bag Mrs. Klein had packed for her. She took a pale yellow sundress and some clean underwear into the tiny bathroom and changed before washing her face and brushing her teeth. She was just pulling her hair up into a braid when Jackson knocked on the door.

"Morning, Holly," he said through the glossy wood. "The car's here and I've made us some coffee."

She opened the door to see him buttoning up a short-sleeved shirt over a pair of shorts. His casual approach in certain situations was still almost mind-blowing. As Holly watched him repack his things into his suitcase, she felt a tightness in her chest. These little moments with him, doing these everyday things most people wouldn't think about, was almost too much for her. And when he turned, sensing her presence, he smiled, melting her heart completely.

***

"Hey," Holly said, looking fresh-faced and ready for vacation. He liked yellow on her; it complemented her rosy skin and blonde hair.

"Hey, yourself." He held out a cup to her. "Light and sweet, as you like it."

She took a sip and he watched her shoulders visually relax as she deeply inhaled the French roast. They collected whatever items they'd used the night before and shoved them into their bags before sitting and buckling themselves in.

She held her coffee tightly as she peered out the small window, watching the ground rise to meet them. "The water's so blue! It's just like on TV."

"Just wait until you see it in person."

"Oh, shit," Holly groaned, turning to look at him. "I don't have any bathing suits in New York! Mrs. Klein couldn't pack what I didn't have."

"Don't worry about a thing, Holly." He knew she didn't have many beach-related things and was thankful he had called ahead to the resort to have a personal shopper select some clothes and bathing suits for her. "Vacation is all about living easy."

Holly looked as if she didn't believe him, but she looked back out the window, sipping her coffee as the wheels touched the runway. When the jet had taxied off the runway and stopped before the small airport, Jackson took her hand and helped her through the plane and onto the tarmac. A white convertible sat waiting for them, sent by the resort.

Holly grinned. "Is that our car?"

"Sure is."

She squealed a bit and ran over, the hem of her dress dancing around her upper thigh. "This is so exciting! I've never been in a convertible before."

"Do they not have cars in Michigan?" He laughed, pulling a shopping bag from the back seat. "Here, something to get you started on our vacation."

Inside, she found a pair of sunglasses, tortoise shell and large, just like the ones she wore at home. "Love them."

Jackson opened the passenger side door for her but she bypassed him, snatching the keys from his hand and hopping into the driver's seat. She settled herself in and the engine roared to life. She lowered her shades and peered up at him playfully. "Are you going to get in, or am I vacationing without you?"

"You don't know where you're going," he pointed out, taking a seat and shutting the door behind him.

Holly shrugged. "It's an island. There's only so far I can go before I hit water. Live a little."

The Non-Disclosure Agreement

Jackson laughed as she drove off the tarmac and onto the busy streets of Bridgetown. He had to admit, her slow evolution from a reserved secretary to the sassy siren who called the shots turned him on. He couldn't wait until he got her into the villa and out of her sundress.

"Turn here," he ordered. "Then, don't stop until you reach the beach."

Jackson watched as she sped down the highway, loose strands of golden hair whipping her cheeks. She had a smile that widened when the resort came into view. The Sandpiper was one of the most secluded spots in Barbados. Jackson had to outbid an oil sheik for the top villa at the last minute. He knew he overpaid, but he wanted to impress.

"Is this our hotel?" Holly pulled up next to the main resort building.

"Sort of." He left the car and helped her out as a valet greeted them and took the keys.

A broad shouldered man in a pale cream-colored suit welcomed them, handing them each a mimosa topped with fresh fruit. "Mr. Cantrell, thank you so much for choosing the Sandpiper. I hope you and Ms. McIntyre enjoy your stay with us."

Jackson took holly's hand and they followed the host to a waiting golf cart. Holly giggled a bit. "We need a ride through the lobby and up the elevator?"

"We're not staying here," he whispered into her hair.

She turned to him, brows furrowed. "Then where are we staying?"

"You'll see."

***

Holly couldn't believe her eyes as the host stopped the cart before a long, wooden pier. He handed Jackson a pair of keycards and left them at the base, their feet sinking into the white sands. She looked out over the calm teal waters, seeing a little hut at the end of the slip.

"No way," she breathed as they began their walk down the pier and toward the exotic cottage. "*That's* where we're staying?"

"Yes." Jackson grinned, pulling a pair of aviator shades from his pocket and slipping them on. "It's the best on the island, completely secluded."

The hut was immaculately clean. A large, white, four-poster bed sat in the middle of the room, which had a tempered glass floor. Holly stepped on it carefully, looking down at the blue ocean, the coral visible beneath the clear water. She felt as if she were walking on water and it made her slightly uneasy. On the bed were a number of bathing suits, beach cover-ups, sun hats, sunglasses, and sandals—many more items than were really needed for a three-day stay.

"What do you want to do first?" Jackson asked, opening up some of the windows and letting the ocean breeze in.

"I don't know." Holly took long strides to the bed and hopped on, feeling like a child playing 'hot lava.' "This is just so much." She put her empty glass on the nightstand and sifted through the bathing suits.

"If you don't like them, I'll have them send

more." Jackson came up behind her, wrapping his arms around her chest. "I want you to have everything you need here."

"Everything's remarkable." It was true; the only thing that could've made it better was if it hadn't been a lie. Holly pushed the thoughts from her mind, trying to focus on the picture-perfect vacation. Living in the present was much more enjoyable than worrying about the future.

"I'm glad." He went to the balcony. "The water's nearing ninety degrees. How about I order us some breakfast and we take a dip while we wait?"

Holly nodded and grabbed a white bikini from the bed, then went to the bathroom to change. The bathroom had the same glass floor and Holly gingerly took wide steps to get close to the vanity. She was just getting comfortable with the glass, but as she saw the little fish darting around beneath her, she was once again unsettled. Living on the edge of Lake Michigan had made her a little uneasy about any large bodies of open water. She knew how dangerous it could be, swallowing up ships in a moment and drowning unsuspecting swimmers the next. She had a fear-based respect.

When she left the bathroom, a bottle of sunscreen in hand, Jackson had already changed into his own bathing suit. The dark green bottoms settled low on his hips and the dimples of his tanned lower back were fully visible as he leaned over the edge of the railing. Holly smiled, thinking about how he was totally hers for three days.

"Ready?" he asked, looking over his shoulders at her.

She held out the bottle. "I've already done my front. Can you take care of my back?" Holly smirked a bit as he grinned in return. She was eager to have his hands on her, no matter how innocently it began.

He massaged the lotion on her shoulders as she held her hair up, his hands skimming her body, dipping low on her back and sliding under the edge of her string bikini. Holly leaned into his touch and knew he'd already covered her exposed skin more than enough.

Jackson put his mouth against her neck and whispered, "Ready for a swim?"

Holly sighed as her back touched his chest and his hands slipped over her stomach and under her breasts. Jackson picked her up. She half expected him to carry her to bed and ravish her, but instead he stepped over to the edge of the pier and jumped into the clear water below.

***

Jackson laughed as Holly rose to the surface, drenched and smiling.

"I'm glad I was already in my bathing suit," she said, pushing her hair off her cheeks.

"I asked if you were ready for a swim."

Holly swam to the ladder. Holding on with one hand, she splashed at him with the other. "You never even asked if I *could* swim."

Jackson paused. He *hadn't* asked that. "I'm so sorry, I just assumed…"

She grinned, slapping water at him. "I grew up

on an *island,* you idiot. *Of course* I can swim!"

He grimaced and swam toward her, gripping the end of the ladder. Holly looked out into the ocean, her lips turned up in happiness, her legs churning beneath the sea. He sneaked a peak down at her full breasts, rising above the water. The white top clung to her, outlining each minute curve and was now nearly transparent as it soaked in the water. Jackson felt himself harden and he made a mental note to leave a generous tip to the resort staff who'd made their purchases

"Can I help you with something?" Holly asked evenly, pointing at her face. "My eyes are up here."

Jackson cleared his throat, embarrassed at being caught gawking like a schoolboy. He glanced up at her face, seeing her brows raised in amusement. It was clear she didn't mind his interest. He even thought she pushed her hair away from her chest to give him a better view, or it may have just been a coincidence.

"Maybe," he replied, putting an arm around her waist and drawing her against him. The strings of her bikini brushed his fingers and he fought the urge to pull the cord.

"What's that?" She put a hand at the back of his head.

He pressed his lips against hers, pleased when she moaned into his mouth. His hand drifted up to her breast and she wrapped her legs around his hips. Jackson groaned as she grinded against his erection. Her nipple hardened against his palm.

"God, Holly, I need you," he rasped against her neck as she thrust her hips again.

Jackson knew they were secluded. All other villas were a great distance away, and besides, it was still too early for the prying eyes of even the earliest riser. Feeling brave, he untied her bikini top with a flick of his hand, freeing her breasts. His breath caught in his throat as her chest came into view. He had seen them swathed in silk dresses and lace bras, but seeing them, feeling them, in their natural state was unworldly.

"Stop staring." Holly blushed, starting to cover herself back up.

"No, don't. I just can't help myself. You're so perfect."

His mouth found hers again and he briefly wondered how he could get her up to bed without breaking the friction between them. But the spell was broken anyway when he heard movement above them.

"What's that?" Holly hissed, looking around the water for her top.

Jackson held it out to her, helping her tie the back. "Breakfast," he grumbled, following her up the ladder. He had never been so disappointed by a waterfront meal in his life.

Chapter Eleven

The day passed quickly. They went jet skiing, swam with dolphins by the shore, and ended the afternoon on a secluded beach, the white sands setting the scene. Holly stretched out on a lounge chair, her slowly tanning body sparsely covered by a new, bright red bikini that matched her manicure. A pair of large black sunglasses and a white sunhat made her look like an heiress on vacation, or maybe like a model in a resort ad. Jackson was glad she had her eyes closed and wasn't aware of his blatant staring.

The sun had just begun to set and he'd ordered a barbeque set up on their private plot of land. Now a waiter, chef, and bartender were at attendance, their stations carefully set up by a team of employees. Jackson thought the addition of a flower-lined table and tea lights in the sand made for a romantic setting.

"Still staring?" Holly asked, her eyes closed behind her Dolce and Gabana shades.

Jackson was taken aback. "I wasn't staring."

181

"Yes, you were," she said, peering over the top of her glasses at him, a smirk on her lips. "Considering the attention you've given me today, maybe you won't chicken out tonight."

His mouth flopped open as she replaced her shades and adjusted her top, making her breasts sway invitingly. He knew she was talking about the sexual tension that just wouldn't stop. They had explored each other's bodies, but hadn't fully consummated their mutual attraction. He hadn't wanted to jeopardize their working relationship, but found it almost impossible to say no to her. There'd been more than one night in which Jackson had to take matters into his own hands while thinking about his hired fiancée.

"Sir." The waiter interrupted his impure thoughts. "Your dinner is served."

Holly pulled on a black cover-up. "I'm starving."

"Good," Jackson replied, walking her to the table and helping her into her seat. "I've had them set a bit of everything out for you."

He watched her as she excitedly popped a fresh scallop in her mouth, her naturally cherry-red lips curled into a satisfied grin. "This is so delicious."

The bartender popped a bottle of champagne, pouring it at their table. This completed the dinner. Surrounded by glowing lights, their area lit by the orange and purple glow of the setting sun, made the whole thing picturesque. Jackson couldn't have planned a better start to what he hoped would be an eventful evening.

***

The Non-Disclosure Agreement

Holly was happier than she ever thought possible. As they walked back to their hut hand-in-hand, she wondered if it would be the night they gave in to their desires. She knew he would let her take control, but she almost wished that *he* would be the one to take charge with her, without needling and overt seduction with moves straight out of a trashy romance novel.

As they approached the villa, Holly could see a warm glow emanating from within. "Did we leave a light on?"

"No," he answered simply, opening the door with a swipe of his card.

Holly gasped as she saw the inside of their hut. Every available surface was covered in tea lights and rose petals. Several vases of tropical flowers sat on their nightstand and a bottle of champagne was in a chiller beside the bed. She pushed the fire hazard thoughts from her mind and turned to Jackson.

"Did you do this?" She felt tears of emotion pool in her eyes.

He smiled and gave her a non-committal shrug. "I ordered it, if that's what you mean."

"It's beautiful."

"You're beautiful," he replied, closing the door and bringing her to the edge of the bed. "It's been so hard not to take you. There were so many times I just wanted to bend you over my desk and fuck you in my office. Or other times when I wanted to memorize every piece of your body, taking my time with each part of you."

Holly swallowed, feeling herself grow aroused as

he spoke, his hands skimming her sides through the cotton of her cover-up. She tried to answer him back, to say something witty, moving, stirring, but she couldn't find the words. All her life she was never at a loss for things to say, but in that moment with him, before the line that was so eloquently written in their non-disclosure agreement, she couldn't find a single thing to say.

He took the hat and glasses from her hand, dropping them to the floor. Her cover-up followed, swiftly pulled over her head. Her breasts strained against her bikini top, and although she longed to rip it off and give him full access, Holly also ached for him to be the one to slowly undress her.

Jackson kissed her softly, his hands at the tie on her neck. "Are you okay?"

"Very," she whispered, bringing her hands to his bare chest.

Her top fell to the ground but his mouth quickly took its place as they dropped into bed together, tangling in the pristine white sheets. Holly felt his hardness pressing into her thigh and she groped downward, clutching it through his shorts. He let out a deep groan and found the strings that held her bikini bottoms closed, biting at her neck. When his finger dipped into her softening core, Holly almost came undone.

"Now." Holly sighed, her thighs holding his hand in place, writhing beneath his attention. "I need you. *Now*."

Jackson nipped at her collarbone. "Slow down. We have all night."

"I've been waiting weeks for this. Making me

wait more is just plain cruel."

"I've been told I'm a cruel man," he told her, pulling his shorts down, letting his cock free from the fabric. "But I can't say no to you."

Their lips joined as he hovered above her, her legs spread and her breath held tight in her chest. When he entered her in one solid motion, Holly felt herself grip around him. She let out a small moan of approval. She knew that having sex with him would be amazing, but she didn't know how perfect it would feel with him inside her.

"Please," she begged when he didn't move. "Keep going."

Jackson groaned, cupping her breast. "You're too gorgeous. I can't handle your body right now."

"Fuck me," Holly cried out, digging her nails into his back. She had thought she would be able to allow him to take control, but she couldn't wait any longer. After weeks of anticipation and half-finished moments, Holly seriously lacked patience.

She pushed him off, onto his back, and flew atop him, straddling his slim hips. With her in charge, Jackson's hands were free to explore her body, a fact that Holly sincerely loved. She slowly lowered herself onto him, each delicious inch sending her closer to the edge. His fingers pressed into her hips and her name left his lips in ecstasy on more than one occasion until he was fully sheathed within her.

Holly began picking up speed, willing Jackson to touch her. He cupped her breast with one hand, the other running down the length of her body until settling upon her entrance, putting a delicious pressure upon the tiny pearl hidden within her folds.

Kelsey McKnight

When Holly felt she couldn't take any more, she let herself fall over the brink to unexplainable ecstasy. The waves of pleasure washed over her and she felt him release as well. The unfamiliar feeling of him coming inside her was wildly erotic, making her want more and more.

"That was…so…" Jackson panted when she fell beside him. He leaned on one elbow and ran a finger from her sex-plumped lips to her breast. She heaved upward, craving his touch again. "It was amazing, Holly."

"It was." She almost let out a purr of delight when his hand circled her sensitive peaks. When his thumb grazed her nipple roughly she let out a short cry. "Again," she ordered, squirming when his teeth replaced his fingers. "No." Holly pulled him upward. "Fuck me again."

Chapter Twelve

Jackson smiled as he dropped anchor, looking down at the clear waters. He could see a school of bright yellow fish dart past the propellers. Holly grinned as she joined him at the railing, almost buzzing with an excitement that Jackson found contagious.

"It's so pretty." She sighed, watching the vibrant schools dart through the coral reef below.

"Want to get a closer look?" He bent down to a box behind the captain's chair, pulling out two new snorkel kits and two sets of flippers.

"I've never snorkeled before."

Jackson shrugged, passing her a mesh bag of gear. "You'll love it, I promise."

Holly stuck the flippers on her feet and tightened a mask around her face. "Attractive." The tube in her mouth muffled her voice comically.

He laughed, but still thought she cut a fine figure in her black string bikini, even with the bulky mask. "Adorable."

Jackson was first in the water. He pulled the

ladder of the large pontoon boat down after him. "Come on, the water's great."

Holly bit her lip, adjusting her goggles for the fifth time. "Are we going to get eaten by sharks, or something?"

"Nah. Everything in these reefs is so tame from all the tourists. Besides, there aren't any big sharks in this area."

"Comforting." She sat on the edge of the diving dock and gingerly dipped her feet in the water. "Just don't let me die, okay?"

"Come on, Holly, it's just a bit of water. You grew up on Lake Michigan!"

"Yeah, a *lake*, Jackson. Not an ocean." She eased herself into the water. "I've never even *seen* the ocean before this."

Jackson's eyes widened. He remembered her saying she hadn't been on vacation much, but he hadn't considered she'd never been to the beach or swam in salt water. "Fair point. Well, I promise you won't die. People snorkel around here all the time. Once you get into it, you won't regret it." He pulled his mark over his face. "Just follow me."

He dipped under the gentle waves, looking back as Holly joined him, awkwardly but steadily, trailing at a short distance. He slowed up to swim beside her and he spied an octopus beside a rocky outcropping. The creature seemed rather uninterested in them, making it safe for a closer look, its arms waving. Jackson pointed down before taking a deep breath and diving toward the bottom. He motioned for Holly to join him. When she dove down alongside him, Jackson noticed she did so without hesitation, apparently growing comfortable with the latest pursuit.

Once the octopus had retreated back to its hideaway, Jackson swam upward, pleased as Holly surfaced, her face split in a wide smile. "Feel better about this?"

"This is amazing," she gushed. "Let's go look for more! I want to see a starfish and some giant conches and some little seahorses." Without waiting, she replaced her mouthpiece and dunked back under.

Jackson hurriedly followed. As they swam at a short distance, he kept glancing in her direction. She paused, surrounded by a hoard of silvery fish. With her hair floating around her head and a group of aquatic creatures at her hips, she looked like a mermaid. Jackson thought she'd look rather nice in a seashell bra.

He turned away, scanning the ocean floor for a conch shell. Although they couldn't take the shell from the reef, Jackson at least wanted to bring her one to see up close. He spied an empty cream-colored shell at the bottom. He shot down and scooped it up, speeding up to the surface to show Holly.

The water was tranquil and eerily empty without the telltale bubbles and splashes of a snorkeler.

"Holly?" Jackson called out. No one answered.

He dipped back below sea level and scanned the reef. The terrain was ragged with high bunches of coral and low, rocky caves. Jackson's heart began to race as he swam, his head whipping from side to side, searching for any trace of her. He prayed she was just exploring, holding her breath as she investigated a cluster of starfish and not trapped in an underwater tunnel.

But as a group of blue fish cleared his view, he saw her, her mask gone, golden hair floating in the current. Her body was limp, but her arms waved unnervingly with the current. Holly wasn't moving.

Jackson powered toward her, ripping off his cumbersome mask. When he reached her lifeless form, he tried to yank her upward, but her foot was caught. The strap of her flipper was hooked on a bent rock. He leaned downward, pulling her foot free and dragged her to the surface. When they hit air, he willed Holly to cough, breath, anything, but her lips were blue and he didn't feel any movement in her chest.

As he pulled her wilted body onto the diving deck, he cursed his selfish decision to set out without a crew. He thought the pontoon would be prime for snorkeling, as well as getting some alone time out in the ocean. But now he swore he'd never be so self-centered again. He had driven boats countless times, taken the proper safety course, but he had never performed CPR on a real person.

His hands shook as he tried to remember what he'd learned in his middle school boating class. When he couldn't think straight, he began pressing on her chest, recalling an episode of a medical drama he'd watched. Her body was cold and he felt an odd sense of guilt as he banged on her breastbone, worried he would hurt her, although Jackson knew it was his only chance to save her life.

"Please, Holly, please!" Jackson gritted his teeth and took a breath, blowing air into Holly's lungs. "Come on, baby, breathe." He repeated the motion several times, growing more terrified at each passing moment. The likelihood of brain damage, if she lived, was becoming more plausible with every passing second.

Holly suddenly opened her eyes and turned over, violently coughing up seawater, emptying her lungs. Jackson grabbed a towel and wrapped it around her shaking shoulders as she heaved in deep breaths. He silently thanked the heavens as she sobbed into his chest, his arms tight around her.

"Are you okay?" he asked, petting the wet hair from her cheeks.

"I'm okay," Holly coughed and answered, her voice raspy. "I just wanted to see...there was a weird long fish...its teeth...it snapped at me."

"Probably a barracuda," Jackson said, pulling back to look into Holly's face. "Are you sure you're all right? I'll radio back to the resort for a medical team to meet us at the docks.

She shook her head and tried to stand. "I'm fine. I don't want to go back."

"Holly, you could have *died*. You need to see a doctor." His voice wasn't as firm as he would have liked, but he helped her up to the main deck and into a large cabana lounge.

Holly flopped back onto the sheets, her breathing slowly dropping back to its normal pace. "I'm okay now. I just want to lay here for a while. Thank you for saving me."

Jackson pressed his lips to her forehead. "I

promised I wouldn't let you die."

She smiled wryly. "At least you're a man of your word."

"Are you positive you feel all right?" He reached into a mini fridge next to the lounger and passed Holly some water.

"Yes." She adjusted herself against the pillows and rubbed at her chest. "Ow. I think I'm going to bruise tomorrow."

Jackson sat beside her, taking her hand. "I'm sorry."

"Don't be," she said, closing her eyes. "I feel very *Sandy* right now."

"Sandy?" He repeated quietly. He briefly wondered if she was disoriented from oxygen loss.

"Yes. This whole thing is very *Danny Zuko* of you."

"You're talking nonsense." Jackson began to seriously worry, as it was clear to him that Holly had forgotten his name. He reached over for the radio. "We're going back to shore."

Holly's eyes snapped open. "You don't know who Danny Zuko is? Jackson, you might be the businessman in this relationship, but you have a hell of a lot to learn about quality film."

Chapter Thirteen

"Back in the real world." Jackson sighed when they'd dropped their bags in their New York City bedroom. Three days hadn't been sufficient, but by the way they explored each other's bodies during that limited time, Jackson knew there'd never be enough time in the world.

"It's nice to be home again."

Jackson smiled at the sound of her calling it home. "It is."

Holly plugged in her phone, long dead since their arrival in Barbados. When it turned on, she let out a small shriek. "We're everywhere!"

"What?" Jackson asked, unbuttoning his shirt for a shower.

She turned the phone toward him. The front picture on some celebrity website was a full cover shot of them tangled on the deck of the pontoon boat. Jackson could remember that moment clearly. These pictures were taken the second day of their trip, when he'd saved Holly from the reef. Thankfully, whenever these pictures had been taken, it was after she'd finished coughing up the water.

"Nice." He tossed his discarded shirt in the hamper and made his way to the bathroom.

"Amber texted me. They say we're the new *Brangelina*." Holly giggled, her fingers tapping at the screen.

"What the hell does that mean?"

"They like us," she explained. "Or at least, the magazines do. Have you talked to your campaign manager today about the polls?"

"Honestly, I haven't spoken to him since before we left for Barbados." Jackson didn't even want to look at his phone. The whole time they were gone, his cell buzzed almost nonstop until it died. He was sure the office could handle itself, but obviously Denny needed some attention. "I guess I need to give him a call."

Holly looked at him peculiarly. "Who are you and what have you done with my boss?"

He paused. "What do you mean?"

"You went from having a full datebook of meetings and business calls to dropping everything so you can fly to get fresh seafood." Holly brushed her hair away from her tanned face. "Quite the change."

"Actually, I picked Barbados so I could see you in a bikini." He could tell by her laugh that she didn't believe him. Jackson pulled his phone from his bag and turned it on, greeted by several voicemails, dozens of missed calls, and too many texts to count. Deciding to bite the bullet, he pressed Denny's speed dial.

Denny answered on the first ring. "Jackson! What the hell?"

"I've been in Barbados," Jackson replied, watching as Holly slipped into the bathroom to shower, stealing his spot. He hoped he could cut the call short and join her.

"I know that. All of America knows that...you beautiful, gorgeous, toned god of a man!"

Jackson's jaw fell open, shocked that his doom and gloom manager sounded so positive. "You sound pleased."

"Because I am! You're a goddamn *genius*!"

"For going on vacation?" Jackson asked as he took off his watch and kicked his shoes to a corner.

"Yes!" Denny laughed aloud. "You and that girl looked so in love even *I* was convinced. She's one hell of an actress, and so are you! This is probably the smartest thing you've done this whole campaign."

"I'm going to be honest. This wasn't the reaction I saw coming."

"Because you're usually so obtuse. But your vacation, was pure genius. These pictures are gold." Jackson could hear the sounds of flipping papers and assumed Denny had a stack of magazines before him. "Men want to be you, women want to be with you, and the whole time, in all of these pictures, you don't take your eyes off this girl. If I didn't know you better, I would think you're really in love with her."

"Really?" Jackson ran a hand through his hair. He needed to get hold of some of those gossip rags and see what the public saw.

"Yes. They love you. The business made you look smart and competent, but the way you look at this girl, with total devotion, makes you look like a *nice guy*. Voters are eating it up!"

Jackson was at a loss for words. Sure, he liked the way Holly looked, but was it so blatantly obvious he had more than just passing feelings for her? It had been a while since he'd felt the true pangs of a lovesick heart, but Jackson thought maybe he felt more for her than he cared to admit.

***

Holly rinsed the shampoo from her hair, taking her time as she showered. The previous few days filled her mind. Everything from the days out in the warm, blue, waters to the nights spent in bed were almost too good to be true. In fact, they *were* too good to be true. She fought back emotions as she remembered why she was there in the first place: to be a good actress.

She sighed and turned off the water, wrapping a towel around her chest. When they boarded the private jet for home, emblazoned with Jackson's company logo, she felt wretched. Once they landed back in New York, she knew the game was back on and the fun was over. But she couldn't let go. Not really.

When she crossed back to the bedroom, dressed for bed with her damp hair in a braid, Jackson was waiting, his eyes upon her. "You all right?" he asked as she slipped between the sheets.

"I'm fine," she answered, turning the lamp off

quickly. Holly thought she could handle having a placid expression, but she was obviously wrong. She wasn't sure whether or not she wanted to address the storm of conflicted feelings swarming in her chest.

"Sad to be back in your sprawling New York City penthouse among the staff and unlimited riches at your disposal?" he jested, gathering her in his arms.

She knew, at that moment, she had to get it all out in the open. "Can I be honest?" Holly traced his collarbone, gathering her strength.

"Of course."

"This is really hard. Extremely hard."

"I've got something hard for you," he growled in response, grabbing her hips.

Holly tried to control her giggles and stay serious, but in an instant, he cut through her depressed demeanor. "I'm trying to talk to you and you're only thinking about your genitalia."

"To be fair, I'm thinking about yours, too." Jackson tugged at the end of her nightie playfully.

"I'm serious." She laughed, almost all solemn thoughts fleeing her mind. Holly fought to grasp them again, sitting up and flipping the light back on. "Jackson, stop thinking with your little head and hear me out."

"Okay, no prick talk," he said, giving her his full attention.

"I was saying this is becoming difficult for me." Holly averted her eyes from his nude torso, settling her focus on the Degas he had hung on the other side of the room from their bed. "I know this started as a job, but I'm having trouble finding the line anymore."

"So am I," he admitted, running his hands through his hair the way he did when he was thinking, or felt torn. His lips were pursed thoughtfully as he watched her.

"I don't know what's going on, but I don't want to get hurt."

"Holly." He rose beside her. "I don't want to hurt you. I *won't* hurt you."

His words stuck her in the chest, creating a tight sensation she could hardly handle. "I want to believe you."

"Then believe me." He took her hand, kissing her knuckles. "I want you here with me, employed or otherwise."

"Do you mean that?"

Jackson nodded. "I do. I really enjoy our time together. You've changed me, Holly. Before you, I would've never left work without notice and spent a few days off the grid. You're beautiful and you make me laugh. I haven't laughed, really laughed, in so long. I didn't realize what I was missing until you came in and dumped finance reports all over my office floor."

Holly choked back her emotion, which threatened to overflow. All the negative baggage that came with thinking about their arrangement melted, leaving her heart warm. "Is that how you really feel?"

"I've lied to my mother, and all of America, but I've never lied to you."

Chapter Fourteen

When Jackson entered the event space that evening, it had been completely transformed. The usually sterile white area was lit with blood red lights. Ragged black tablecloths covered the many tables. Giant spider webs made of tattered white lace covered the high ceilings, and acrobats in spider costumes spun on thin ropes above the guests' heads. A live band played dramatic music as dry ice fog flooded the dance floor and women dressed as witches passed out alcoholic concoctions that resembled blood in evil-looking goblets. The guests were dressed in all sorts of expensive costumes from Egyptian pharaohs to werewolves with animatronic jaws. He was highly impressed.

He wandered around the room, looking for his mother and Holly. He assumed Ursula was waiting to make some ridiculous grand entrance, but he thought he would at least see Holly greeting the guests or playing hostess in some other way. He thought he spied Amber dressed as a zombie cheerleader, flirting with a vampire, but he couldn't be sure. As he kept his eyes open for his assistant-turned-fiancée in the crowd, he decided to acknowledge some of his mother's friends—a flock of cougars scantily dressed as cats in bikinis following a sexy nurse who was passing out cootie shots.

"Little Jackson! Is that you?" Pricilla, his mother's oldest friend, planted a kiss on his cheek. "You look so handsome dressed as Batman. I hardly recognized you."

"Thanks, Pricilla. Holly picked it out," he said, shifting uncomfortably in his spandex suit.

"She sure has good taste." Another woman, Kathy, purred in appreciation of the way the tight fabric showed off his muscular form.

"Where is your fiancée?" Pricilla asked. "I haven't had the pleasure of meeting her and I heard she planned this party."

"She did." Jackson felt a strange sense of pride in her achievement. "Holly's very creative, so I knew she would organize something amazing."

Kathy's gaze flitted over to the cobweb-rimmed stairs as a spotlight brightened, drawing Jackson's attention to the balcony above. A figure stepped out of the shadows and he felt as though his heart had stopped. Holly stood at the top of the stairs, her blonde hair curled and wild in a sexy way that made her look freshly bedded. She wore a bright green, strapless leotard that showed off her impeccable figure and a set of pale green thigh-high stockings that ended in a pair of emerald high heels. Ivy leaves wrapped around her long legs and hugged her supple torso and bare arms. A few small red roses with green leaves were artfully arranged in her hair to make an earthy crown. It was obvious she was playing the comic villain Poison Ivy and that's why she wanted him to be Batman. He smiled at her cleverness as she began to speak.

"Good evening, ladies and gentlemen." Holly's voice abruptly ended the music and forced all attention to her. "I am Holly McIntyre and I am so pleased that you're able to join the Cantrell family tonight in celebrating the birthday of the fabulous Ursula Gaspar-Cantrell. Now, please turn your attention to the far corner of the room and join me in welcoming the queen of the evening!"

Holly waved a hand dramatically to the other side of the room where a spotlight illuminated a figure entering from the darkness. Ursula was perched on a golden swing that slowly lowered her to the ground from the ceiling. Her large powdered wig and colorful voluminous dress reminded Jackson of a strange, exotic bird although he knew she aimed to be Marie Antoinette. He was clapping for his mother's entrance when he felt a hand on his shoulder.

"Hey, you found your costume." Holly had snuck down from the stairs as everyone's attention was focused on Ursula.

"You look amazing, incredible...perfect," Jackson said, admiring her closely. Her intimate proximity gave him a chance to appreciate the vivid green eye makeup accentuated by small green jewels and brilliant red lipstick that framed her pearly white teeth.

"You don't think it's too much?" she asked,

biting her lip in an appealing manner.

Jackson shook his head, momentarily amazed that the rapid movement hadn't made his mask fly off. "Why would I think it's too much? It's fantastic. Also, I like how you placed us as mortal enemies. Very smart."

"I thought it would be funny, and I've always had a soft spot for Poison Ivy. She was so misunderstood. Have you had a chance to look around at all?"

"A bit. I think it's great what you've done to this place. You're really talented, Holly. And I can tell my mother loves it."

"I hope so. I have specially cocktails and imported candy gift bags as favors. I also decided that, instead of dinner, it would just be desserts to go along with Marie Antoinette's favorite things. I found some French baker I saw once on the cooking channel to make cake and tiny desserts. There's also a professional photographer to follow Ursula around, a costume contest to be judged by your mother, and a special surprise at the end of the night." She grinned mischievously, looking more like her villain character by the moment.

"What's the surprise?"

"If I told you, it wouldn't be much of a surprise."

"Come on, Holly, I won't tell," he pleaded, clasping his hands together dramatically.

She shook her head, her curls bouncing. "No way, Batman. But do you want to see her birthday cake?"

"Of course." He held out his hand, allowing her to lead the way to the back kitchen. As they passed through the swinging doors, Jackson peeled off the Batman mask so he could fully see the cake Holly had ordered.

A huge baked confection stood before them on a florally decorated cart, waiting to be rolled into the event space. It was ten towering layers of white icing and decorated with colorful sugar flowers and birds scattered throughout. Thick, classical candles were spread on the tiers in even intervals. It had been made to resemble one of Marie Antoinette's famous powdered wigs. Trays of cupcake with equally elaborate icing, yet in darker shades to mimic the décor, surrounded the impressive centerpiece.

"Do you like it?" Holly asked, a shy smile playing on her lips.

Jackson felt so overwhelmed that he took her in his arms. "Everything is perfect. This space, this party, these costumes, this cake, you—they're all so utterly perfect."

She blushed, turning her head away from him to hide her reddening cheeks. "It's not a big deal. I was happy to do it for your mom."

"Don't turn away from me, Holly. You need to learn how to take a complement."

She whipped her head back toward him in defiance. "I can take a complement just fine."

"I like Poison Ivy, Holly. She's so full of life, just like you."

"I'm hardly full of life."

"You are," he told her. "You're so much like her. You're strong, enchanting, and your kisses are like poison."

"Actually, only her first kiss is poisonous. The second one acts as an antidote. If you read the comics—"

He leaned down and gave her a light kiss on her blood red lips, silencing her. After a moment, he added, "It looks like I'll just have to take another."

They moved toward each other, both caught up in the moment. Their lips were about to touch when the door flung open to reveal Pricilla, grinning a sly smile. "Come on, you lovebirds, Ursula has been looking for you everywhere."

"You owe me," Jackson whispered in Holly's ear as they followed Pricilla into the crowd.

Ursula screeched when they entered her line of sight. "A toast! A toast!" She called, lifting a smoking cocktail in the air, urging the partygoers to be silent. "I want to make a toast to my new *fille*! To my beautiful future daughter for putting on this soiree and inviting all you lovely people to celebrate. She is the little girl I never had but am thankful to welcome into my family. To Holly!"

"To Holly!" The guests mimicked loudly then continued their celebrations.

Jackson watched as Holly's face lit up with pride. Although she tried to put on a modest front, she enjoyed getting the recognition her hard work rightly deserved.

He scooped her up, dragging her the dance floor. The band pumped out fast paced songs and soon the both of them were caught up in the crowd, drinking medicinal looking shots from miniature beakers and spinning in each other's arms. Holly's primal attire and carefree expression made her shin in a new light that Jackson didn't know she had. As the night progressed, he found himself deeper, and deeper, under her spell.

When the time came for her special surprise, Holly left Jackson and climbed on stage with the band. She grabbed the microphone and cleared her throat before addressing the crowd. "Good evening, everyone! I hope you all are having a lovely time at Ursula's birthday?"

The masses roared in the affirmative.

"If everyone would please follow me outside to the terrace, there is something fabulous awaiting." She replaced the microphone and nimbly jumped off the stage, heading toward the large doors that lead to the outside. Jackson was frozen to the spot watching her sashay from the room. It seemed that she kept surprising him from every angle.

The night was cold and it took Jackson a few moments to find Holly in the throng of people all looking up at the sky over the city. She stood with his mother against the railing, looking out into the darkness with a smile on her face. "Hey, there you are." He came up behind Holly, hugging her from behind in an attempt to warm her arms.

She leaned back on his chest. "Just keep watching the sky."

Suddenly there was a loud boom, making the guest jump and shriek. The sky lit up with fireworks in all the colors of the rainbow. Short blue bursts, long red streaks, and brilliant pink flashes brightened the city. Jackson tore his eyes from the display to look down at Holly's face. Her eyes were bright and her lips were parted in a look of pure delight. She clutched at his arms and laughed. Jackson felt a peculiar tightness in his chest but chose to ignore it, deciding to keep his eyes on the woman before him who'd brought so much happiness into his life.

***

"That was so much fun. And I'm so happy your mom liked everything," Holly said, picking the wilting leaves out of her hair and throwing them out of the limousine's open window.

"She *loved* everything. All of her friends are dying to have you plan all their events now. You're a very popular woman, Miss McIntyre," Jackson teased.

"Good. No offence, Mr. Cantrell, but being your personal assistant wasn't my ultimate career goal." She giggled, propping her feet up on the limo seats. While her shoes were adorable, hours of dancing, walking, and hopping around had made her long to kick them off.

"I don't blame you. You've been working overtime since we got back from Barbados. I wish we could just relax tomorrow, but I need to go into the office and work on my final campaign dinner."

Holly frowned. "Do you really? It's Saturday."

"I have to go to work and take care of my girls, don't I? I'll only be in a few hours then maybe we can get lunch or something."

"Good. That would be nice. Maybe we could go to the Natural History Museum?" she asked hopefully. "I've never been there before and with all this craziness going on, I haven't had a chance to cross anything else off my New York City bucket list."

"If that's what you want, I can meet you there after my meetings."

"That would be amazing," she said, gazing out into the night.

For the first time in a while, Holly felt at ease with her life. Jackson had spilled his feelings to her, and they seemed to be a flawless match in goals and desires. Being together was so wonderfully uncomplicated that she couldn't believe her luck. He made her feel cherished and adored. She hated to be a sappy romantic, but he treated her like an absolute princess.

Once they were back at the apartment, Jackson helped her out of the car and, silently, they made their way up to the penthouse. The earlier promise of a second kiss hung in the air and Holly could almost taste the delicious tension between them. In the private elevator he held her gently at his side, slowly skimming his fingers up and down the tendril of ivy wrapped around her bodice.

"Jackson," Holly said, but Jackson cut her off with a passionate kiss that she felt from the roots of her hair to the points of her toes.

"Oh, god, Holly. I've wanted that all night," he growled into her lips before his mouth covered hers again.

Holly felt his touch emanating heat through her body and they barely made it into the bedroom before she fully gave into her desires. Her body was alight with feelings; longing, need, dare she even say love? The thought was pushed far from her mind when they landed on the large bed together, grasping each other like lifejackets in the open water. His hands explored her body, slowly unwinding the leafy vines that surrounded her shape. The roses in her hair began to break, scattering petals on the sheets.

Jackson unzipped his costume and allowed it to fall to the floor before fumbling with Holly's outfit, searching for a zipper or buttons. "How the hell do you get this thing off?"

She rolled her eyes and slipped the strapless leotard off in one easy moment. "Men are so simple," she joked, her eyes locked on Jackson's body, which was clad only in a pair of tight boxer briefs that accentuated his slim hips and the bulge beneath. Holly was left in a strapless black bra and matching panties as well as her bright stockings and sky-high heels.

"You're so gorgeous," he breathed, taking her in his arms again. "You get more beautiful each time I see you."

His lips searched her body, making their way from the curve of her neck to the swell of her breasts. Her breath held in her throat as Jackson cupped one heavy mound in his hand and began gently teasing her peak with his thumb, making her moan in pleasure. He glanced up at her, shooting her a dimpled grin. His mouth fell on her body again and teased its way down her stomach. Holly felt goose bumps prickle her skin and she could hardly remember ever being so turned on. When his mouth touched the lace edge of her underwear, she gasped, waiting for something more. But Jackson passed over the strips of silk and resumed his attentions at the top of her stocking.

"You have the most amazing legs, Holly." He sat up, lifted her shapely calf and gently removed her shoes, tossing them on the floor. Then he began unrolling her thigh-highs in a deliciously slow manner. As each inch of pale skin was revealed, he placed a light kiss on the fresh patch.

"Come back up here," Holly pleaded, reaching up for him.

He smiled at her, placing his lips against the curve of her foot before beginning on her other leg. "So impatient. I've been waiting for this all night and now it's your turn to wait."

"That's not fair! At first you were all like, *'Wah, we can't do this. Put your heaving bosoms back into your shirt. I'm your boss! Wah, wah, wah!'* And now you want me to wait?" she asked, a jeweled-accented brow raised. "It's not like we haven't already had sex before."

Jackson laughed. "I can see how that might be seen as unfair," he said, stripping her other leg of her stocking. "But who said life was fair?"

When Holly's legs were bare, he lowered himself onto the bed beside her. He traced her lips with the tip of his finger before dropping his hand behind her, unhooking her bra. Her breasts fell free and he cupped them eagerly in his hands, caressing the smooth skin and making her sigh in pleasure. Jackson pulled her body under his, positioning herself between her legs. She felt his hard member grinding against her, making heat pool at the juncture of her thighs. Holly clasped his shoulders and lifted her hips toward him, willing him to take her.

"Please, Jackson, I need you," she whispered in his ear, making him groan.

"God, Holly, you'll make come right now." Jackson pushed himself up on his elbows and smoothed her panties off, leaving her delectably bare for his appreciation. He slowly eased his hand down, toward her slit, forcing her to endure a delicious wait. Gradually, he palmed her, teasing her gently as a soft whimper escaped her lips. When he slipped a finger inside her, she let out a sharp cry of desire. "You're so wet," Jackson said in her ear, taking off his boxers.

Holly felt her heart begin to race as she waited for him to enter her. The torture of wanting him so badly was driving her insane and she longed to join herself with him. Between his work and her party planning, they hadn't had a moment alone since Barbados. When he pulled his boxers down, she grasped his hips, waiting for the moment that he fully entered her. "Please," she whispered, softly pulling him toward her.

His eyes met hers and in a single movement he filled her completely, making them both shudder. Jackson slowly began pumping in and out of her tight body, groaning with each inch. Holly's nails lightly scraped his back and her mews of contentment turned into sexy moans as he picked up the pace. When she felt Jackson empty himself into her, she allowed herself to fall into orgasmic bliss, crying his name into the darkness.

The Non-Disclosure Agreement

***

The next morning, Holly awoke enclosed in a pair of strong, male arms. Jackson pulled her into his hard body and his even breath against the nape of her neck told her he was still asleep. She smiled and ran her hand along his, curled in sleep against her breast. She lifted each perfectly formed finger and inspected it.

"Everything up to your liking?" Jackson murmured suddenly, making Holly jump.

She blushed and dropped his hand. "Sorry. I didn't mean to wake you."

"It's okay." He placed a kiss on her bare shoulder, his morning stubble scratching her skin. "I need to get up early, anyway."

"Stay here instead."

Jackson groaned and untangled himself from the sheets. "I need to go to work."

"No you don't," she countered, grabbing his arm and attempting to pull him back in the bed.

He leaned down and gave her a swift kiss on the forehead. "I'll make a deal with you. Ill get out of the office by noon and I'll meet you back here. You just stay in bed and continue being gorgeous."

Holly watched him retreat into the bathroom to begin getting ready, and she leaned back against the pillows. Her mouth slid into a smile of total satisfaction at the thought of the previous night's events. The sexy man now bathing himself in the next room had just been in bed with her, promising another night of pure bliss. Her lips tingled with the remembrance of his teeth grazing her skin.

Unwilling to lie in bed any longer, she decided to make Jackson breakfast before he left for the office. She clipped her thick hair up and away from her face, then donned her favorite leopard print bathrobe. The house was quiet and she was happy to see that Mrs. Klein wasn't bustling around in the kitchen. Holly cheerfully began making scrambled eggs and pulling slabs of bacon out of the refrigerator.

For a moment, she paused and wondered if this is what her life would be like now. If there would be long, passionate nights with Jackson and breakfasts together in the morning. If he would run home after his meetings to see her every day. If she would grow to be used to this lifestyle. There were a lot of uncertainties, but they were all positive and gave Holly something to smile about as she cooked his breakfast.

As she finished buttering the toast and filling plates with food for herself and Jackson, he wandered in with a broad smile on his face. He pinched a piece of bacon from a plate. "This is great, Holly. You're quite the little cook."

"Thanks. I thought you might want something to eat before work."

He took the plates and led the way into the dining room. "Well, I did work up quite an appetite last night."

Holly reddened and followed him, holding two cups of coffee. "Jackson, hush! Your mother is here."

"Yes, I am," a voice said from behind her. "Lovely party last night, Holly."

She turned and came face to face with Ursula, who wore a feather-lined silk robe and artful makeup. "Ursula, I didn't expect you to be awake. Would you like something to eat?"

"No, no, no, darling. I will die if I eat anything before bed."

"You didn't sleep yet?" Holly asked as they sat at the table.

The older woman shook her head. "Of course not. I never sleep on my birthday. There is too much to do."

"I'm glad you had fun last night, Mother," Jackson said between bites.

"Ooh, yes," Ursula purred. "It was perfect. I cannot wait until your wedding! It will be fantastic. Everyone who is anyone will be there to see my new daughter."

"We haven't even really planned anything yet," Holly mumbled, taking a bite of toast, not feeling very hungry all of a sudden.

"Well, there needs to be an engagement party. Everyone needs to meet you first," Ursula said. "I was telling my dear friend Pricilla how much needs to be planned and she was very worried that I would tire myself out, but I must tell you, I feel much younger."

"That's good. You need to rest more," Jackson said.

Ursula waved him off and took Holly's hand in hers. "*Ma chère*, these last few weeks of getting to know you has been the best since my poor husband passed. I want to thank you for what you've done for myself and my little boy."

"Oh, no need to thank me." Holly bit her lip, unsure of what to say.

"I've always wanted a little girl of my own. You have become the daughter I always wanted." Ursula stood and planted a light kiss on Holly's forehead. "You are perfect, *ma chère,* and I am so pleased you are joining our family."

Jackson and Holly watched as she sauntered down the hall toward her bedroom. They exchanged guilty looks and Holly pushed her plate away. Being spoken to so nicely by Ursula and knowing she thought of her like a daughter created a sick feeling of guilt in the pit of her stomach.

"Jackson, can we go into the bedroom? We need to talk."

He stood and looked at her grimly. "The most dreaded words in the human vernacular."

"I can't do this anymore," Holly hissed at Jackson once they were safely behind the closed door of his bedroom. "Your mother trusts me!"

Jackson sat on the edge of the bed, running his hands through his hair. "I know. I feel terrible, but that was basically the whole point of this."

"We need to tell her. We can't keep lying to her."

"No."

"Jackson," Holly whispered, sitting next to him on the bed, "this is getting out of hand. We'll just tell her and keep it a secret with the three of us until after your election. We're going to stay together, anyway, so I don't see the harm."

"I can't. We're in too deeply now. We need to see this through." She placed a hand on his knee and squeezed the firm muscles beneath his slacks as Jackson continued. "Holly, I don't want to lie to my mother, but I can't back out of this now."

"I can't do this anymore. I can't lie to your mom for another minute. I really respect her and I don't want to hurt her anymore." Holly bit her lip nervously. She didn't think she would have some a moral issue with lying to Ursula, but as time went on, she'd begun to see her as a mother figure. "She'll understand why we lied. I'm going to tell her today."

Jackson shot up and turned on her, his icy eyes boring into her. "No," he said through gritted teeth. "You won't say a word to her. If you tell her the truth, she'll never forgive me. She hates being lied to."

Holly cowered slightly. "But I can't lie to her anymore. She says she thinks of me as a daughter."

"Well, you're my *assistant* and I'm *paying* you to pretend to be my fiancée, so just keep on pretending," he retorted sharply, sucking the air from Holly's lungs. "Just remember this is your *job*, and don't screw it up by breaking your non-disclosure agreement."

She stared at him, her eyes wide and her mouth parted in shock. "Jackson—"

"Just keep your mouth shut." He picked up his briefcase and left the room, closing the door harshly behind him.

***

He'd been too hard on her; he knew that. He

hadn't meant to be so cruel. It had been an act in the beginning, but she'd opened up a new part of him he wasn't aware existed. They took walks in the park together, went on trips, attended events as the perfect couple everyone else envied. But he'd let his selfishness and his lies jeopardize his budding relationship with her.

Now, as he sat in his stark office, he found it almost impossible to pay attention to his paperwork or participate fully in his meetings. All he could think about was Holly's willingness to keep everyone around her happy and the wretched look in her eyes as he slammed the door behind him. It was in stark contrast to the sensual woman with the lively features who'd writhed below him the night before.

"Jessica!" Jackson barked, collecting the papers from his desk and shoving them into his briefcase.

"Yes, sir?" Jackson's new assistant, a short redhead, stepped into the room. He hadn't planned on hiring anyone new, but when it seemed like Holly might end up playing the part of his lover forever, he needed to fill the gap in the payroll. She had been working for him for several weeks and proved to be a very good assistant—when she wasn't spending too much time on Facebook.

"Cancel everything for the rest of the day. I need to get home at once."

"But…sir, these meetings took weeks to put together. I don't know if I'll be able to reschedule them." Jessica paled.

"No matter. There's something of great importance I need to take care of. Make something up. Either way, I'm going home."

***

"Holly?" Jackson called as he entered the apartment. He dropped his coat and briefcase on the floor and adjusted the giant bushel of roses in his hands. Making his way toward the bedroom, he noted the apartment was eerily silent. He'd grown so accustomed to hearing something that reminded him of her as soon as he came through the front door—music blasting in the living room, or the sound of her cooking and laughing with Mrs. Klein in the kitchen.

He knocked gently on the bedroom door. "Holly?" When he didn't receive an answer, he slowly let himself into a spotless, empty room.

Jackson frowned and dropped the flowers on the dresser before checking the bathroom. The countertops where Holly's makeup and perfumes had been meticulously lined up were bare. The shower only held his personal items. Her robe was missing from the hook behind the door. Feeling his blood run cold, he ran to the closet and threw open the doors. His suits were lined up on the racks but the rest of the closet was empty. No dainty heels or billowy dresses lined the vacant walls and even the drawers were completely unfilled.

All she seemed to leave behind was her engagement ring, which sat alone on an end table, glittering forlornly in the afternoon sunlight. Jackson picked it up with a shaking hand, his mind spinning. He couldn't believe she left—wouldn't believe it.

He dashed to the old guest room, where Holly had spent her first night, hoping she'd just moved her things back there to punish him for his ridiculous outburst. But the guest room was also empty. "Damn it, Holly," Jackson growled, sitting on the bed and placing his head in his hands. "What the hell have I done?"

"Yes, my son." His mother's voice purred from the open doorway. "What have you done?"

Jackson looked up to see her leaning against the doorframe, a lit cigarette in her hand and an unhappy look on her face. "Do you know where she is?" he asked.

"No. I came home from an appointment to see her moving her things out. Another girl was helping her. Holly was obviously upset and wouldn't say a single thing to me. She did say she was sorry." She narrowed her eyes and held out her hand, showing him the diamond ring he'd given Holly. "She also gave me this. Now tell me what you have done."

"I said something nasty to her that I'm afraid I can't take back. It was totally inexcusable."

"What was it?" Her eyes narrowed. "Tell me what you did."

He'd bought out companies, fired hundreds of people, given speeches to thousands, yet he could barely form the words he needed to say. "It's about Holly."

"Obviously."

"She's not really my fiancée."

"What do you mean?"

"She used to work as my assistant. When the

election came closer, my manager and I thought…"

"Go on." Ursula's voice was cold and her eyes said she knew what her son was about to say.

"I hired Holly to pretend. I needed to look like a family man to the voters and—I know it's stupid—but I wanted you to see that I was serious about politics and that I wasn't just some guy banging pop stars on yachts."

"You are joking, no? You did not ask her to pretend anything. Tell me you have not done this terrible thing."

Jackson squared his jaw. "I did. I've been paying her this whole time."

She slowly placed the butt of her cigarette in an ashtray. Then she brought her hand up and slapped Jackson on the back of the head. "You idiot! You have ruined *everything*!"

"But I did this for you. For the company and the Cantrell name!"

"No. You go to boring lunches for me. You stand outside the dressing room and hold my purse for me. You pretend to like my friends for me. You did not do this thing for me. What you have done is cruel to me, that girl, and especially yourself. Why would you do such a stupid thing?"

"I wanted to give you something to look forward to and something to be proud of." He dropped onto the couch next to her and put his head in his hands. "Dad build this company, I only helped it grow. Politics was going to be my legacy."

Ursula magically produced another cigarette and lighter from the sleeve of her Japanese-inspired robe. "I've been on board with your political aspirations for weeks now."

He looked up at her, confusion obvious on his face. "You have? But you spent years telling me how pointless it was."

"Yes, but Holly convinced me otherwise."

"She did?"

"We have grown quite close." She took a drag, exhaling the smoke delicately before continuing. "She cares for you. And I'm not sure exactly what went on with you two, but it is obvious you have hurt her greatly."

Jackson cringed. "I know. And I think I really screwed it up."

"Well, aren't we the clever one?"

"I'm not in the mood for your sarcasm, Mother. I really ruined everything and now I don't know what to do to fix this."

"You be a man. You were taught that having money and fame and things were what makes you a man. You thought that once your father died and you got the company, then you would finally be a man. But no, you are a man when you find a woman who exposes you for what you really are and helps you be the man you were meant to be. Now, stop being a silly child and go find her."

Chapter Fifteen

Holly pulled her sweater tighter around her and picked at the smooth stones on the beach. She tossed a few into the gently lapping waters of the lake. She'd been home at her parents' house for only two days, and so far everyone had mercifully left her alone. Even her sister, who was normally so meddlesome, allowed Holly room to grieve.

When she first pulled up to the farmhouse in one of Mackinac Island's golf carts, her parents came out smiling, expecting to see her with their future son-in-law in tow. Instead, they saw a lonely, sniveling daughter and mounds of luggage. Holly didn't have to say a word before her mother enveloped her in a soft hug and her father asked her cheerfully if she was interested in some dinner. They hadn't asked a single question of her since.

Now, she was unsure of what to do. She was back where she started in her parents' home without any prospects for the future and a thoroughly broken heart. She thought things had changed between her and her boss. He was so tender and made her feel like the most desirable woman in the world. They shared deep feelings and a final, perfect night together. The next morning, he was strictly business without any care for her feelings. Holly felt a sharp pain in her chest as she remembered how his usually kind eyes glared at her with distain as he left for work. Where she thought they were officially lovers with a future, he decided that they were merely coworkers and she was just another conquest.

Angrily, she picked up another handful of rocks and threw them into the water before stomping back to the house. When she opened the back door, she saw a familiar young man sitting at the kitchen table with her parents. In a rush, she remembered all the times she'd held his hand, ran her fingers over his chest, and kissed his face—which she now fought the urge to punch.

"Brian, what are you doing here?"

Her high school boyfriend, Brian, rose to his feet as he smoothed back his light-colored hair and grinned at her. That playful smile had made her melt once, but she was a different person then. "I heard you moved back to Mackinac and I thought it would be nice to stop by."

"Okay." Holly crossed her arms over her chest and waited for more as Brian shifted nervously where he stood. Holly's parents slowly slipped out of the kitchen to give them some privacy. "What do you want?"

"I can't just come and see you?"

"Not after you were such a jerk to me."

He sighed. "I know I have no right to be here or

even talk to you, but I just needed to do this. Seeing you in all those magazine looking so happy with that other guy made me jealous."

"You came all the way here to say that you were jealous?"

"Yes, I did." He took a step closer to her. "I hated seeing you with him, knowing that I officially lost you."

Holly scoffed, thoroughly annoyed that Brian had decided to try to squirm into her good graces. "You officially lost me when you slept with that other girl. I would say that totally ended our relationship."

"I know, and I'm really sorry about that. It was a stupid mistake."

"Whatever, Brian. I think it's time you leave." She turned to the fridge and opened it, pulling out a bottle of water. "Bye, now."

Brian held out his arms, his face contorted in an exaggerated pout that made him look ridiculous to her, rather than sympathetic. "Just hear me out. I know I did something terrible and I deserved to lose you, but when I heard that you broke up with that guy in New York, I saw it as the universe giving me another chance at happiness with you."

She rolled her eyes. "I seriously doubt the universe wants you anywhere near me."

"Ew!" A voice behind them let out a terrible gagging noise. "What's *he* doing here?"

Holly turned to see her little sister, Kara, walking into the kitchen with her faithful cat, Bo, trotting behind her. "I was trying to find out the same thing."

"Hello, Kara," Brian muttered, dropping his arms to his side.

"Brian. It's *so* good to see you again." Her voice oozed sarcasm. "Are you here for tea? To pick up a catering order from my parents? Or to screw with my sister's life a little more?"

Brian sighed again, playing the part of the victim. "I just came to apologize to Holly and try to make her see that I'm really sorry. I was young and selfish. I've had time to grow and change over the past year, and I want to fix things." Despite her reluctance, he took Holly's hands in his and gazed at her with his chocolate-colored eyes. "Please, Holly, give me another shot? Just one date to see if you feel anything at all for me."

"You can't be serious," Kara spat. "Why can't you just leave her alone?"

"Because I think we have a real chance."

"Ugh. Whatever." Kara rolled her eyes and disappeared around the corner, fed up with his dramatic display.

"If you actually came back here with the intentions of getting back together, you're seriously deranged," Holly told him, pulling her hands from his sweaty palms.

"Just one night. That's all I'm asking. Think about all the plans we had. Taking over your parents' restaurant one day, having a couple of kids, maybe going to Europe. Isn't that what you always wanted?"

She frowned, remembering the long nights they'd spent out on the beach talking about a future that seemed perfect in every way at the time. "It was," she admitted.

"I can give you all those things, Holly. I know I made a huge mistake, but I want to make things right and see if there's anything left for us."

Jackson's face flashed in her mind, but Holly pushed it aside. "I just got out of a relationship. I don't think I'm ready to get into something serious right now. And I really don't think I'd ever want to get into anything with *you*."

Brian sighed and grabbed his jacket from where it hung, draped over the back of a chair. "I understand. I just wanted you to know that you I'm here for you if you ever want to go out or just be friends." He reached into his pocket and pulled a business card for his accounting practice from his wallet. "Here, my cell number is on the back. Call me if you ever want to get together."

***

When Holly came home from work the next afternoon, she found Kara sprawled on the living room couch, a tabloid magazine open in front of her. Her brow was creased and she seemed to be studying something intently.

"Anything good?" Holly asked, peeking over the top of Kara's head.

Kara shot up, crumpling the magazine in her hand. "No!" she shouted, putting the tabloid behind her back.

"Are you okay?"

"Yeah, never better," Kara said with a short, unnatural laugh.

Holly narrowed her eyes and inspected her jumpy sister. "What's going on?"

"Nothing!"

"Is there something in that magazine that I need to see?"

Kara averted her gaze. "No."

She felt her chest tighten. Kara certainly wouldn't be acting so strangely for no reason. "It's him, isn't it? Just tell me."

Her little sister paused as if unsure of what to do before flipping through the crinkled pages and stopping at a spread of pictures. "I just saw it and I wasn't sure if I should show you or not. I wanted you to see it before anyone else had the chance to, but I didn't know how."

Holly's mouth went dry as she took the magazine. There, in full color, was a picture of Jackson looking dapper in a tuxedo. At his side was a gorgeous brunette with full red lips and a matching couture gown. His arm was around the brunette's waist and he was leaning over to whisper something in her bejeweled ear. It looked quite intimate. Holly could barely force herself to read the short article that followed.

Masterful mogul Jackson Cantrell is single and ready to mingle! After a quiet break up from fiancée Holly McIntyre, it looks like New York City's most eligible bachelor has his sights set on actress Jennifer Good. The two were seen getting cozy at the premier of Good's new movie, "The Stranger's Kiss." Sources close to Good say that the two lovebirds are getting serious and are already talking marriage and babies. Billionaire hottie Jackson certainly got over that small town girl fast!

Holly shut the magazine and passed it back to Kara before sitting down slowly next to her on the couch. It felt as if a great lump had settled into her chest and she wasn't sure if she wanted to cry, scream, disappear, or all of the above. "He's got a new girlfriend?"

"It might not be true." Kara bit her lip and placed a hand on Holly's knee. "They print stuff that isn't true in these magazines all the time."

"It probably is. I spent the first few weeks working for him dodging calls from models and actresses he was involved with. This girl is just his type." Holly fought back nausea as her brain began replaying images of Jackson and Jennifer before her eyes.

She'd seen Jennifer Good in several movies and magazines, and the woman was classically stunning. She also spent her free time in Africa building schools and donated money to children's hospitals all down the east coast of the United States. Beautiful, rich, *and* a philanthropist—Jennifer Good was everything Holly wasn't and she hated her for it.

"I'm sorry, Holly." Kara looked at her sorrowfully. "I shouldn't have let you see it."

"No. You did the right thing. I needed to see it." She rose from her seat. "I'm going upstairs. I'll talk to you later."

She went up to her room and closed the door

behind her before letting the tears fall freely. The hot, frustrated tears embarrassed her. She felt as if she had no right to cry over a taken man, no matter how intimate they had once been. After all, he had made it clear from the beginning that it was all just business. It was her who had gotten caught up in things.

She stalked around her room, looking at all the moving boxes she hadn't unpacked yet. They were full to the brim with designer shoes and expensive dresses, gifts from a man who didn't love her and never would.

Seeing those things that Jackson had given her made her angry. He'd tried to buy her off and now he was talking about getting serious with another woman. Holly wiped the wetness from her cheeks with the back of her hand and went to her desk. Brian's business card lay on the edge. Sure, Brian hadn't been the best boyfriend, but he had never broken her heart as deeply as Jackson did. He seemed honestly sorry for ruining their relationship and didn't even push for her forgiveness as hard as she thought he might. Brian was also here waiting for her while Jackson was dating a leggy actress with a killer smile.

Fighting back spiteful tears, Holly picked up the business card and pulled her cellphone from her pocket. The phone only rang once before she heard Brian's voice on the other line.

Chapter Sixteen

"This stuff is so awesome," Kara gushed, gently stroking an expensive bag like a beloved pet. "I'm glad you took it with you."

Holly looked down at the gold embossed leather that held such good memories of her time with Jackson. She had carried it almost every day and it was something special he'd bought her as a gift. "Keep it."

"You can't be serious. This is a really expensive bag. Normal people don't have this stuff."

"I need to get rid of it all. Besides, where am I going?" Holly asked despondently, flopping down on her bed amidst the piles of designer fashions she had recently unpacked at the request of her sister. "I'll be working in the restaurant when I'm old and wrinkly. I don't have any use for this stuff anymore. Take it all to college with you. You're bound to need some fancy stuff for job interviews and homecoming or something."

Kara frowned and sat down on the floor next to Holly's bed and began opening shoeboxes. "He was a huge jerk, but at least he had good taste."

"Yeah, always the fashion icon." Holly whispered sarcastically, feeling a sharp pain in her heart. She briefly wondered if Jackson and Jennifer had gone shopping for her movie premier together and quickly buried the thought in her mind.

"You don't have to say anything if you don't want to, but I think it might help you to talk about him."

"It's really complicated, Kara. I don't think you'd understand."

Kara raised her eyebrows, dropping a pair of shoes back into their box. "I'm old enough to vote, go to war, *and* star in a porno. You can talk to me like an adult."

Holly cracked a small smile. It was so easy to forget that her little sister was so grown up sometimes. "Well, you know I went down there for a job? I ended up working for Jackson Cantrell as his assistant, first. It was pretty basic stuff for a while until he came up with this plan to trick the public into thinking he was some family man."

"He thought that having a girlfriend would make him win an election?"

"Yeah. That's why he hired me."

"You can't be serious. You were being *paid* to date him? Paid to go shopping? Paid to go to fancy dinners? No way." She shook her head, her brows furrowed. "No one is that lucky. It sounds like a movie plot."

"Like *Pretty Woman*?" Holly asked wryly, remembering that conversation in Jackson's office many weeks before.

"Exactly like *Pretty Woman*. But is that why you're here? Did he fire you or something?"

"Not exactly. I was stupid and thought that there was more to our arrangement…more *feeling*. At least, what's what I thought was happening. I thought he was beginning to…." She shook her head. "I was just really dumb and I have no one to blame for my stupidity but myself."

"You're not stupid." Kara moved to sit next to Holly. "You really cared about him."

Holly felt her eyes well up and angrily fought them back. She had spent days sobbing in secret and she wasn't keen on breaking down in front of her little sister. "I did and I thought he cared about me too, until the other morning. I threw this party for his mom and we were living together—Jackson and I—and one thing led to another and I had feelings for him. I thought about it before Barbados, but when we were there, just completely alone with each other, I knew I felt deeply for him. He even saved my life."

"He saved your life?"

"Yeah." She sniffled. "We were snorkeling and I got caught up in something. He pulled me out and gave me CPR. I would have drowned if not for him."

"What happened then?"

"I got overwhelmed and said I wanted to stop lying to his mom and come clean about the whole thing. He freaked and told me to do what I was hired for. He threw our arrangement in my face."

Kara shook her head and took one of Holly's hands in her smaller one and gave it a quick squeeze. "Wow, that's harsh. What a jerk."

"No, he's not a jerk. He shouldn't lie to his mom, but it wasn't my place to make that decision for him. I mean, what did I think telling his mom would change? I was wrong and he was right. I was being paid to play a part and when my services were no longer welcomed, I left."

"What are you going to do now?"

"I don't know. I guess just live here and work with mom and dad. I need to get back into my old life. I've even decided to meet Brian for dinner."

Kara instantly released her hand and flopped back against the pillows. "Ugh. Don't go out with that loser again, he was a total jackass."

"He's older now, Kara. I just want to see if he's any different." Holly knew her words were basically a lie and she had no real desire to see Brian again. She forced a small smile.

"Or he might be exactly the same."

"I know, but I'm going to give him the benefit of the doubt and just have dinner with him. I need to move on from Jackson and this is just a small step to getting over him and getting back out there."

"Holly, you just got out of a relationship."

"It wasn't a relationship." Holly felt another painful pang as she said those words aloud. "It wasn't a relationship at all."

***

"I'm really glad you agreed to come to dinner." Brian smiled over the tea candles clustered in the center of the table. He wore a smart suit without a

232

tie and his grin was stretched a mile wide. "I was almost afraid you wouldn't come."

Holly smiled tightly, trying to relax. They sat together in one of nicer restaurants on the island and it almost felt like she was back in her old life before New York. She was even wearing one of her familiar dresses from high school—a pale pink tea dress with white laced trim. Everything about the piano music, candlelight, and black-tie waiters made Holly feel like she was on the perfect date.

If only Jackson was here. Holly shook the thought from her mind and tried to turn her attention back to Brian.

"So…" He searched for something to say. "Glad to be back in Michigan?"

"I'm going to miss New York City, but it is kind of nice to be back home."

"It's too bad you missed being here in the summer and came back right in time for winter. You missed a great fall festival too."

"I was going to come home for Christmas, anyway," she said absently, rearranging the already perfect silverware.

"Maybe we could do something for the holidays like we used to. Go out and find our own tree to put up back at my place, or maybe go ice skating? You always used to love going ice skating on Christmas Eve."

Holly *did* love those little holiday traditions they used to share. But looking over the table at Brian made her feel some level of resentment toward those once cherished traditions. Was she really going to be happy living in the same house, working at the same restaurant, marrying the same man, and living the same life? Sure, it was comfortable, but it was also exactly what she was trying to escape when she left Michigan in the first place.

"So, what do you think?" Brian asked, jarring Holly from her thoughts.

"About what?"

He looked at her strangely. "About going camping with my brother and his wife next weekend. I want to get out to the woods again before it gets too cold."

Holly blinked several times as she processed his words. She could hardly believe what she was hearing. It almost made her laugh. "Camping? Brian, I thought we were only doing one dinner. That doesn't mean that I'm ready to go as your date to all family functions."

"You're right," he said, looking down at his clasped hands. "I'm getting way ahead of myself. I'm just really excited. It's nice to see you, Holly, and I want to at least be friends if you can't forgive me for the mistakes I've made."

"It's nice to see you too…even if you were a huge jerk," she added with a small smile. She could tell he was trying. She couldn't really hate him.

"I know, I know. I'm working on it though. Taking classes, reading self-help books, eating vegan…"

"You're such a liar!" Holly laughed aloud, surprising herself.

He looked at her fondly and reached across the table, putting his hand on hers. "It's really good to hear you laugh again, Holly. I missed it."

"It feels good to laugh again. It's been a while and I've been finding it hard to find the humor in things."

Brian straightened in his seat, his face taking on a mask of exaggerated seriousness. "I accept your challenge."

***

"Holy shit, Holly, I've been waiting for you forever!" Kara sat in the dimly lit kitchen, waiting up for her. "Can't you ever pick up your phone?"

"I told you I was having dinner with Brian and I'm pretty sure I left my phone upstairs in my room." She kicked off her white pumps and sat on the kitchen counter, facing her sister.

"I know you were out with him, but I've been trying to reach you." She bit her lip and toyed with a strand of hair that had fallen from her ponytail.

Holly knew that look and knew it was one of either guilt or fear. "Is everything okay? Are Mom and Dad all right?"

"Jackson was here," Kara blurted before clamping her hand over her mouth.

Holly felt her blood drain from her face and a wave of vicious nausea hit her in the stomach like a punch to the gut. She couldn't believe that Jackson Cantrell had really been in her parents' house. She tried to collect herself and pretend that the thought of him being in the same state as her didn't make her dizzy.

"Why?" she asked simply, pretending to inspect a loose stitch on her hem. She couldn't let her sister

235

see her crumble again. It was becoming far too common.

"He wouldn't say, just that it was really important that he spoke to you. But it sounded really urgent. He wouldn't leave without knowing where you were."

Holly's stomach dropped. "Did you tell him?"

"Yeah." She averted her eyes. "I thought maybe if you guys saw each other—"

"What?" Holly asked, suddenly angry with Kara for butting into her broken love life. "What did you think would happen, Kara? You thought our eyes would lock over a crowded room and he'd fall in love with me and carry me out of the restaurant like it was a movie? Is that what you expected?"

Kara looked down sheepishly. "When you put it like that, it sounds so lame."

"Well, it didn't happen," Holly whispered in a cracked voice. "He didn't come for me. He doesn't care. He probably just came for his apartment key, or something. I accidentally took my set with me when I left."

"I'm sorry, Holly." Kara stood, opening her arms for an embrace. "I thought I was helping."

Holly stepped into the fold of Kara's arms and allowed a few tears to fall down her cheeks. "Don't be sorry, it's not your fault. I thought I was starting to get over him and it's like nothing I do helps. Now I find out he was here and…and I missed him. But he was only probably here for another booty call."

"Don't say that," Kara soothed. "It'll all work out. You don't need that asshole."

A sharp knock on the door made them both

jump. Holly looked at her sister questioningly, but Kara merely shrugged and went over to the door. She peeked through the curtains out onto the darkened porch. She gasped and quickly shut the fabric.

"Who is it?" Holly asked, wiping her tear-streaked face with the back of her hand.

"It's Jackson. What do I do? I think he saw me." She slid down to the floor, her voice a hiss.

Holly felt another fresh wave of lightheadedness and the rapid beating of her fragile heart. She felt as if she might faint and leaned against the counter. "I don't know."

"I can tell him you're not home."

"No, I can't lie to him."

"Why? He lied to you and made you think he was this great catch." Kara crossed her arms. "I can go tell him to screw off."

"You know this door isn't exactly soundproof, right?" Jackson called, his voice muffled.

Holly's face grew hot. "Oh, great. Now there's no hiding. I guess I'll just have to see what he wants."

"Need me to stay?" Kara asked, rising from the floor.

"No, I need to do this alone. Thanks, though." Holly tried to force a brave smile as Kara left the room.

Her hand shook as she unlocked the kitchen door and turned on the porch light. Jackson stood there wearing a pair of jeans and a leather jacket over a white shirt. He had circles under his eyes and his usually cocky demeanor seemed muted, almost defeated. If she wasn't so sure it was him, she might've thought Jackson had a disheveled twin on the loose.

"What do you want?" Holly kept a tight grip on the door to steady herself.

"We need to talk."

"No, Mr. Cantrell," she said in the most businesslike voice she could muster. "We don't have anything to talk about. I'm not working for you anymore. I've moved out all my things, and I'm living back in Michigan. There's nothing more for either of us to say to each other. You obviously know where I live, so just have your secretary send my last paycheck here."

"That's not true. Can I please come in so we can talk?" He looked at her pleadingly, making Holly's heart hurt.

"My parents and sister are here."

"Then can we take a walk or something?"

Holly sighed. "Can't this wait until tomorrow? I'm really not in the mood to talk to you right now."

"No, Holly, this can't wait. I've already waited almost a week to talk to you and I can't wait another night. We're talking now."

Holly felt anger well up inside of her. The kind of bitter anger that only mutates from a broken heart. "You think you can just show up at my home and demand to talk to me after complete radio silence? I'm not your employee anymore and I don't appreciate being treated like one. Besides, I'm not even a good employee, remember?"

Jackson visibly flinched at the reminder of their last conversation. "I'm sorry, I know I have no right to come here. I just didn't know what else to do. Just please take a walk with me."

"Fine, but I need to get changed first." Holly closed the door, not bothering to let Jackson inside. She went up to her room and took off the dress, changing into a pair of jeans and a thick sweater that would shield her from the late fall cold. She pulled on a pair of boots on her way out and even inspected her face for any traces of smeared mascara. Just because she'd been crying didn't mean she needed to look like it. He had moved on quickly and she needed to appear to have done the same.

"Where do you want to walk to?" he asked as Holly pulled the door shut behind her.

"We'll just go down to the beach or something." She started down a path into the dense woods, not waiting for him to follow.

"I thought you said we were going to the beach." He looked at the darkened trees and raised an eyebrow at her.

"We need to go through the woods to get there."

He nodded and shadowed her in silence. Holly almost wished he would walk with her and take her hand in his like he did when they strolled through Central Park. But then she remembered he had a famous new girlfriend and tucked both hands in her pockets to push away the urge. Neither of them spoke until they reached the rocky shoreline. The full moon lit up the still waters of Lake Michigan, and Holly could spot the last nighttime ferry docking on the small island.

"So, what did you need to talk about?" Holly

asked, not bothering to turn and look at him.

"What I said to you that morning after the party. It wasn't right."

"You came all the way to Michigan to tell me something I already know?"

Jackson stepped up beside her and out of the corner of her eye, she could tell he was looking at her. "It's more than that. I've done bad things before. I've bought out small companies and sold the pieces bit by bit, forcing hundreds of people to lose their jobs. I've destroyed my rivals, forcing them into bankruptcy. I've used people—innocent people—to get what I wanted without caring about what it would do to them."

"I'm aware." She crossed her arms over her chest.

"But I never thought in a million years I would treat you like…like…."

"Like an employee? That's what I was, Jackson. You paid me to do a job. I didn't do my job well, and you fired me."

"You were never like an employee to me, Holly."

"More like a prostitute," she grumbled, the words tasting bitter on her lips.

Jackson pulled her to face him, his expression pained. "Don't talk about yourself like that."

"Then what would you call it? You hired me to be your girlfriend, and as soon as I put out, you told me where to shove it."

"I know that's how it all started, but then I really got to know you." He released her arms and ran his hand through his messy hair. "I saw you tonight with that guy and I almost didn't come back."

"What are you talking about?"

"I saw you at dinner with that guy, holding hands and laughing. I used to be him. I used to be the man who made you smile like that."

Holly flushed, thankful that the darkness probably made it impossible for him to tell. "What do you care if I had dinner with somebody else?"

"Because I *need* you, damn it!" he yelled, his voice echoing over the motionless water.

Holly looked up at him, her mouth open in surprise. She wasn't sure if she'd heard him right. "What did you say?"

"I said I need you. I've ruined so many things in my life and I couldn't stand it if I ruined my chance at a life with you, too." He reached out and tucked a blonde strand behind her ear. "I need you, Holly."

"I can't be in some kind of arrangement with you again. I'm not going to do that to myself," she said, trying to ignore the electric shock that hit her the moment his fingertips brushed the side of her face.

"I'm not asking you to go back on the payroll, Holly."

"Then I don't get why you're here. I gave you my body and opened up to you fully, and you treated me like trash." Hot tears welled up in her eyes. "I *trusted* you."

"I know, and I can't tell you how sorry I am for that. I never meant to make you feel like I thought so little of you. I was just trying to protect my mother and I stupidly hurt you in the process. I was a thoughtless asshole and you didn't deserve that. I know I shouldn't expect you to ever forget about

241

what I said to you, but I'm hoping that maybe you could try to forgive me."

"And then what? You want me to be your Michigan state booty call? I'm not going to be one of those girls I used to pity. You know, the ones whose calls I dodged for you back when I worked in your office. It would kill me to have some assistant lie and tell me you were in Hong Kong."

He flinched a bit and grimaced. "I know. It would make you feel how I felt when I saw you out with that other guy tonight."

Holly rolled her eyes, thoroughly angry now. "Are you serious? You threw me away and now you're mad that I was out to dinner? You can't be for real. You've moved on and now I'm trying to do the same."

"I wanted to punch your date right in the face."

"You have no right to be angry at me or judge my decisions. *You're* the one who pushed me away."

"And now I come to find you and you're out to dinner with some other guy!" Jackson nearly shouted.

"You treated me like trash and I never heard from you again. You have all of my information. My phone numbers, my address, even my goddamn social security number, *Mr. Cantrell*. I wasn't exactly in hiding. Now you show up after a week of nothing. Does your girlfriend even know you're here? I know I'd be pretty pissed if my boyfriend was in another state trying to turn his former employee into a fucking mistress."

"I don't want you to be my mistress. Besides,

I—" Jackson shut his mouth and looked at her curiously. "Did you say *girlfriend?*"

Holly rolled her eyes so hard, she was sure she caught a glimpse of her own brain. "Don't play dumb with me, Jackson. You're a public figure. I can't even pass a news stand without seeing you on some cover."

"Holly, I don't have a girlfriend."

"Oh, yeah? I know all about her."

He crossed his arms over the expanse of his chest. "Then tell me what you know, because this mystery girlfriend is news to me."

"Jennifer Good," Holly spat, stalking off to sit on the sand at the edge of the water. It was cold, but Holly felt like if she didn't sit down her knees would collapse under her. She felt emotionally drained.

"Jennifer Good isn't my girlfriend," Jackson called out before coming over to her and sitting next to her in the sand. "She's *just* a friend."

"And I was *just* your assistant." Holly pulled her legs up to her chest and leaned her chin on her knees.

"You were so much more and you still are. I'm *not* dating Jennifer. She helps out with one of my charities when I ask her to. She's a good spokesperson."

"I saw you together in the magazine."

"I'm seen with a lot of people in magazines, Holly. It doesn't always mean I'm dating them."

Holly wanted so badly to believe him, but she didn't want to get herself hurt again. She knew she should have left things then and abandoned the conversation, but she felt frozen in place. "You guys looked really close."

"So did you and that guy at dinner."

"I guess, but if you stalked me to the end of my date you would have seen how it ended."

"Okay, enlighten me."

When she and Brian left dinner, he tried to pull her into a darkened alleyway beside the restaurant. He was apparently hoping for a taste of dessert, but instead Holly delivered a quick knee to his groin before hurrying home. She told Jackson about it.

"Good, he deserved it."

"Yeah, I knew he was a jerk when I agreed to go to dinner, but I thought he would've grown up."

"I'm really glad there isn't anything between you two. Now…come home with me, Holly." His voice was soft and encouraging.

She felt his gaze burning into the side of her face, but she couldn't give in. "I can't."

"Why can't you? We can leave first thing tomorrow and everything can be just like they were before. I'll even take some time off and we'll go somewhere again, just us. You can pick anywhere in the world. France? India? Australia?"

She turned to look at him. His ice blue eyes smoldered and Holly almost wanted to say yes. However, he had shown his true colors and she wouldn't be able to forget it, no matter how much she wished she could.

"Things can *never* be how they were before. What you did was terrible and I can't make myself into your Barbie doll again. I'm not perfect. I'm never going to be comfortable at gala events or be okay with you working long hours at the office. I can't lie to people for you anymore, or always wonder if you really care about me. I can't have you throw the contract in my face every time I disagree with you. I deserve better and I'll wait for better."

Jackson inhaled sharply. "Don't be like that. I know I treated you terribly, but I'm here for you asking you for forgiveness."

Holly dug her fingers into the cold sand and looked back out over the lake. "Took you long enough."

"I needed to sort some things out first. I needed to make myself a better man and take care of my responsibilities before I tried to be worthy of you again."

"Well, at least now you can say you tried, after a whole week of soul searching, and you can go back to your girlfriend with a light conscious."

"She's *not* my girlfriend," he said in frustration.

"Just leave me alone, Jackson."

"Please, Holly, reconsider. I can give you anything you want," he pleaded with her, placing a heavy hand on her arm. "You can redo the apartment so you'll feel more at home. Or we'll buy a new place, wherever you want. You can go to Italy and get the best furniture made. I'll call all my European contacts and have them bring you the best jewelry. Or, better yet, you can go pick everything out and even take your sister. Just tell me what you want and I'll have it done."

"Don't you get it, Jackson?"

"Get what?" He sounded honestly confused.

Holly stood, pulling her arm free. "You haven't

changed at all. You still think you can buy me." She turned and began walking up the beach toward the woods.

"Holly, wait!" Jackson yelled, scrambling up.

She stopped and rotated to meet him. "Just stop, Jackson. I don't want to do this. I don't want houses or jewelry or trips. I never wanted those things. All I ever wanted was you." She turned on her heel and made the long walk back to the house alone with fresh tears streaming down her face, leaving him on the shores of Lake Michigan alone.

Chapter Seventeen

Jackson sat in his office, staring at his computer. An image of him and Holly at his mother's birthday party filled the screen. The photographer had sent the pictures days ago, but Jackson couldn't make himself look. His mother hadn't wasted any time printing, framing, and hanging all the pictures she could find of him and Holly all over the apartment. Ursula had made quite the show of removing everything else from the walls and even hiring art professionals to hang up each enlarged image and calling Jackson to inspect the placement of each item.

He'd started spending as much time as he could at work, trying to ignore his crumbling private life. Three days earlier, he had left Michigan and come home to Ursula chain smoking in his living room, her cold gaze calculating and judgmental. Although she had refused to speak a word to him, she made sure Holly was everywhere he looked. It was the worst punishment she could have dealt.

"Sir?" Jessica popped her head into his office. "I

have the finance minister of Finland on line three."

"Who cares?"

Her eyes widened. "What?"

Jackson stopped, realizing he had spoken aloud. "Nothing. Thank you, Jessica."

He tried getting some work done. He answered some calls, donated some money, tried going over some takeover reports, but found he couldn't focus. By the time Denny called him, Jackson could barely force himself to pick up the phone.

"Jackson. Denny," his campaign manager started. "Have you been looking at your numbers lately?"

"I'd rather not," he replied, tuning away from his computer. Politics was the last thing on his jumbled mind.

"Well, it's shit. Your breakup has really hit you where it hurts and your numbers are low, low, *low*."

Jackson knew the words should have upset him, but he was struggling to find the will to care. "So, it's over?"

"Jackson, buddy, what the hell happened?" Denny's voice had lost its edge. "You were a goddamn shark with this shit and now…nothing. Is this about that Holly girl?"

He leaned back in his seat, looking out at the New York City skyline. "I fucked up."

"Look, I don't know what kinda deal you had going with this girl, but as your manager, you have to level with me now."

"Long story short, she was my assistant, I used her as a fake fiancée, developed feelings for her, then majorly hurt her by treating her like an

248

employce and telling her to just do what I paid her for."

Denny let out a low whistle. "Yeah, I can see why she would hate your guts. But there's no way to salvage it? At least have her come back for the rest of the campaign season?"

"I just got back from Michigan."

"And?"

"She's not coming."

"And whose fault is that? I've seen you tear people apart to get what you want. You've dropped money on yachts just to impress oil sheiks. You've flown clients to China for Chinese food. What did you do for this girl?"

Jackson rubbed his chin, prickly from forgetting to shave that morning. Well, he had gone into the bathroom to do it, but there was a tube of Holly's bright red lipstick right on the counter and he completely forgot all about his scruffy cheeks. "Denny, you're right. I haven't tried hard enough. But she says she doesn't want my money."

"You love her."

Denny's words made him pause. Of course he felt something strong toward Holly, but he'd thought it was merely lust or the first few weeks of a new romance, always full of positive feelings. He never thought to put a word to those feelings, but perhaps Denny was right. Maybe he *did* love Holly.

"Is it obvious?"

Denny chuckled into the receiver. "Well, *I* can tell you do. I work with politicians, and I know how to pick out a lie when I hear one. It's all part of the game."

Jackson sighed. "I really screwed up, Denny. I screwed up and I don't think she'll ever forgive me." He felt a pang in his chest as the words left his lips. The thought of Holly leaving his life for good hurt more than he'd like to admit, but who better to help him fix a messy situation than one of the top campaign managers in the game who had cleaned up much worse during his career. "You have to help me, Denny. I need to get her back."

"Wow, you really got it bad, huh?"

"Can you help me or not? I need to have her forgive me. I want her back."

"Jackson, I would if I could. This isn't some secret mistress or coke habit I can just pay away, this is a real person that you hurt. You say you care about her, so figure your shit out."

Jackson cursed as he hung up the phone. He had to come up with a new plan.

Chapter Eighteen

Kara unwrapped the morning magazine, and newspaper deliveries. "Ouch," she said.

Holly finished opening the shades in the restaurant and looked back at her sister. "What is it?"

"Your ex is bombing this election stuff."

"So?" Holly tried putting on a nonchalant attitude, but she really felt for Jackson. He poured his hopes and dreams into politics and now, probably because of her, he was going to lose.

Kara shrugged and plopped the periodicals into the newsstand. "Sucks to suck. I guess he's just going to have to settle on being a ridiculously handsome business tycoon. Tough life."

Holly didn't respond, but as soon as Kara headed back to open the kitchen, Holly rushed to the newsstand and grabbed *The New York Times*. She set it down on the nearest tabletop, hurriedly scanning the story titled

Billionaire Businessman Bombs Balloting.

251

Jackson Cantrell, Republican nominee for New York City Mayor, has plummeted in the polls. Last week, Cantrell held 79 percent of the popular vote and he is now at a low 23 percent. His opponent—

"I knew you couldn't stop yourself." Kara was leaning on the doorframe of the kitchen, her arms crossed.

"Do you think me leaving is what's costing him this election?" Holly asked, carefully folding up the paper.

"Who knows? Either way, you made it pretty clear it's no longer your problem."

"I can still feel bad for him."

Kara pursed her lips, obviously dying to say something.

"What is it?" Holly asked.

"I just think you're making a mistake."

She rolled her eyes. "Not this again." She turned to unlock the front door for business.

Kara flipped the sign back to *'closed'*. "Yes, this again."

"Kara, there's a lot to this that you don't know and I'm tired of talking about it. Jackson and I are over for good. So, please stop."

Holly busied herself with finishing up the opening measure for the restaurant; ignoring Kara's stern looks her way. It was so easy for her younger sister to think that love was enough to fix what Jackson broke. Of course Holly would have liked nothing more than to fall into his arms and allow him to jet her back to New York. But, life was

252

never that easy.

***

Holly awoke to a loud knock on her bedroom door. She groggily looked at her clock. It was nine on the morning, way too early to be up on a Saturday when she was still holed up, licking her wounds. She slid out of bed and opened the door to find her sister looking at her eagerly.

"What is it?" Holly yawned. "Why are you up so early? Neither of us are working today.

"Just come see." Kara grabbed her hand and tried pulling her into the hallway.

Holly dug in her heels and pulled her hand away. "Kara, I worked late last night. Can't this wait?"

"No way you'd want to wait if you knew what was downstairs."

"Kara, I'm tired."

Her sister groaned. "Stop being like that and just come downstairs."

Holly rolled her eyes and began following Kara through the hallway and down the staircase. The living room was full of vases overflowing with bouquets. Roses, hydrangeas, lilies, daisies, and more that Holly couldn't even identify were in full bloom before her. They sat on all the available surfaces, and there were even more on the majority of the floor. Only a small path allowed access from the stairs to the kitchen. She stopped on the bottom step, taking it all in.

"What the hell is going on?"

"They've been showing up since, like, six this

253

morning," Kara told her. "I think there are maybe sixty vases. I lost count after a while. The poor delivery guy must be so exhausted."

"What are we supposed to do with all these flowers?" Holly asked, briefly imagining how overwhelmed—and pleased—the island's only florist must have been.

"I don't know, but it sure looks awesome."

"Are Mom and Dad having an event at the restaurant tonight?

Kara shook her head. "No, they're for you."

"For me?" Holly picked up a vase and took the little pink card nestled between the petals. It read:

Your brilliant smile makes me melt.

"What the hell is this?"

"Oh, the cards," Kara said, looking around. "I started collecting them, but I must have missed a few."

"They each came with a card?"

"Yeah." She found a stack of them beneath one of the larger vases on the floor and handed them to her. "They all say something different. So sweet."

"Did any of them say who they were from?"

"No, but do you really have to ask?" Kara asked, grinning. "This is so romantic."

Holly didn't want to admit she knew exactly who would do such an ostentatious showing. Most of these flowers weren't in season for months, and no normal person would be able to afford to send thousands of fresh flowers in one day. "Jackson."

"Obviously."

She took the cards and began to flip through them as the doorbell rang again. "More flowers?"

"Probably." Kara climbed over the couch and weaved through the vases to get to the door. She nearly stumbled over a particularly high arrangement of purple blooms. A man stood on the front porch holding a bushel of flowers in his arm. A van was parked in the driveway and Holly could see that more flowers waited inside.

"This is ridiculous," Holly muttered, throwing the pile of cards on the couch. She wasn't going to let Jackson try and buy her off with a bunch of flowers. She went into the kitchen and poured herself a bowl of cereal. She took her time, trying to focus on the chocolaty pieces instead of the garden that had appeared in her living room. She had to admit that she liked the flowers. Holly had always adored the look and smell of the fragrant blooms, and must have mentioned it to Jackson during one of their long nights talking. If he weren't such a prick, she would have leaped for joy. But instead of reading those sweet cards with relish, she was hiding, trying to pretend those floral arrangements weren't beginning to creep into the kitchen as more arrived.

Kara came in some time later, holding a large stack of cards. "I think he just delivered the last of them." She put the cards on the table in front of Holly and sat down.

Holly looked at the cards blankly, unsure of if she wanted to open them or not.

Kara seemed to read her mind. "You should maybe read a few."

"He probably just had his secretary write them."

"Or maybe *he* did. You used to read his notes for work. Don't you know his handwriting?"

"I guess so," Holly admitted, reaching for an envelope. She pulled out the tiny pink card and recognized Jackson's sloping script. After taking a stabilizing breath, she read it aloud.

"The way we fit together when we sleep."

"That's so cute."

Holly reddened and shoved the card back into its envelope. "Shut up." She reached for another but opted not to read it so her sister could hear. In Jackson's familiar script it said:

How beautiful you are in the morning.

She couldn't read any more of them. Holly was afraid she would burst into tears if she did. She had no business feeling anything toward her old boss and would be damned if he tricked her into loving him again.

"I still can't believe he sent you so many flowers. Where did he even find them this time of year?" Kara asked, reaching for the box of cereal and eating it dry by the handful.

Holly shrugged. "Who knows? I think it's weird though."

"Weird how?"

"The last time I heard from him was last week when he stopped by and now he sends me all these flowers. I don't want him to keep doing this kind of stuff forever. It's making it really hard to let go."

"Did you hear a knock?" Kara asked suddenly, her head turning toward the living room. She didn't wait for Holly to answer before rising from the table to answer the door.

"Holly it's for you!" she called a moment later.

"If it's more flowers just put them anywhere."

"There are some boxes. I'll just bring it to you." Kara walked into the kitchen holding three blue boxes topped with white bows. She placed the boxes on the table. "There aren't any cards, just numbers. What do you think are in these?"

"I don't have a clue," Holly said honestly. She lifted up the lid of the box marked with a one and saw a portrait of the two of them sitting in a silver frame. It was from their mock photography session where they reenacted a date, both holding ice cream cones in their hands and genuinely laughing. While she knew that day was about pretending, the laughter they shared wasn't an act. She could clearly see the joy in his face and the love in hers.

Holly waited to see if Kara would say something about the picture, and when she didn't, Holly opened the second box. There was a candid shot of them on their single vacation together. It was taken one night on the beach as they stood together in the shallow waves, the moon bathing them in a pale light that seemed to make them glow upon the white sand and black water. Holly could remember that moment clearly. Jackson had just tucked an exotic flower behind her ear, telling her that there had been nowhere else in the world he would have wanted to be.

Her hands were shaking as she opened the third box, but paused when she saw the frame within was empty. In the place where the picture would go was a handwritten note, instead:

For the future.

She stared at the simple note, the lump in her throat growing with each passing moment and the tears falling unbidden down her cheeks.

"There's a letter," Kara whispered. "It was under the box on the lid."

"Just read it to me," Holly rasped, closing her eyes. "I don't think I can."

"Are you sure?"

Holly nodded, and Kara read it aloud.

My dearest Holly,

I tried staying away from you, to let you go like I promised myself I would. You do deserve more than me. You deserve a man who will not only provide you with every comfort you could ever hope for, but who will also treat you with all of the love and respect that you deserve.

The Non-Disclosure Agreement

I know you said you never wanted anything else from me, but I had to give you two last gifts. The first is a summer garden in the winter to make you smile. One bouquet for each day that I loved you and even more to remind you that I always will. The second is a short representation of us from the pretend, to the real, and to whatever we may be now. And I want there to be a now and a future and everything in between. But if you never respond, I'll resect you, because I know that I don't deserve your forgiveness just as you didn't deserve my scorn.

I love you,

Jackson

Her eyes were hot with tears and her heart felt as if a noose was tightening around it. She looked at her sister, her vision blurry. "Oh, Kara, what do I do?"

"Do you really want my advice?"

"Of course I do. I'm just so lost. Every time I think I'd rid of him, he pulls me back in. I hate him and I love him. I don't know what to do anymore."

"Do you want him or not?"

"I don't know." Holly sobbed now. "I'm just so afraid of being vulnerable again. It just felt so terrible, being thrown away like that."

"Look, I told you from the beginning that Brian was a snake because he was. He was a jerk before you met him, while you dated, and then again when you broke up. He'll never change. But I think Jackson is different. He said something stupid, but it seems like he's really ready to make it work with you."

"But what about Jennifer Good?"

"If he says that he isn't dating her, then maybe you should trust him."

"But he lied to his own mother."

"In his defense, it wasn't for a bad reason. It wasn't so that he could hurt anyone."

"But he hurt *me*," Holly cried, louder than she had meant to.

"But, but, but!" Kara said mockingly. "Enough with that. Decide what you want and go for it. You keep letting things just *happen* to you instead of making your own way. You didn't go to college because you didn't get into your choice school. You didn't stay in New York because of a guy. You ran away from the city to come back to Michigan. You went out with Brian again after he cheated on you because you didn't see any other options. You have options, Holly, all you need to do is decide what you want and go for it. Be brave."

Holly looked at her little sister—really looked at her and admired her for the woman she had grown into. Gone was the little brat who would steal her CDs and lock her out of the house. She was replaced with someone far wiser than her years, and Holly knew she was right.

She only needed to be brave.

Chapter Nineteen

Jackson paced in his dressing room, ignoring his campaign manager's attempts at forcing him to lighten up. It was only two days until Election Day and his popularity hovered in the twenties; too low to secure a win. He knew he should be angry with the voters for being so fickle as to abandon him over a failed engagement, but he knew he deserved it. In fact, he almost welcomed the punishment. His annoyance over the election almost took his mind off of Holly—*almost*.

"Are you even listening to me?" Denny asked, sounding fully exasperated.

"Honestly, no."

Denny rubbed at his temples. "This is your last shot. You have to turn on the charm, make the voters love you again—shake hands, kiss babies, and make some promises. This rally is your last ditch effort."

Jackson glanced at his watch. It was almost time for him to make his appearance, and he could think of nothing he would like to do less than go out and bullshit. "I guess we'd better head up there." He turned to the mirror and straightened his red tie.

"Just…try not to screw this up, all right?" Denny slapped him on the shoulder and opened the dressing room door.

Together they strode down the hall in the backspace of the Javits Center's north building. Jackson could hear the murmur of the crowd as they approached the recently erected stage. The crowd sounded more excited; their voices higher and jovial in nature than he had expected. He wondered, for a brief moment, if that was a good thing.

As they reached the stage, Denny twitched the curtain aside. But when he did, his mouth gaped open. "What the hell?"

"What?" Jackson asked with a sigh. "Are there protestors?"

"Protesters I would expect, this is something else."

Jackson shoved Denny out of the way and looked out onto the stage. There was Holly, seated on the edge of the platform, legs swinging casually beneath a bright red tea-dress. She spoke to the reporters at the front without a microphone, making it impossible for Jackson to hear what she was saying. But, whatever it was made the journalists and photographers laugh along with her and Holly's familiar red-lipped mouth split into a wide grin.

"Christ, Jackson! You didn't tell me she was coming," Denny hissed.

"Because I didn't know." Jackson's eyes were glued to her. His heart pounded in his ears as she turned. She must have sensed his arrival.

Chapter Twenty

Holly sat crossed-legged on the bed in her hotel room. She sipped at her iced coffee, feeling awkward and exposed. As soon as Jackson's political rally was over, she told him to meet her there in an hour. When he finally arrived, her favorite Starbucks drink in tow, she was waiting in a Juicy sweat suit, her hair in a ponytail.

When he came in, he immediately attempted to pull her into another embrace, but Holly held out her hand. "I think we need to talk, first."

"Of course." Jackson nodded, but Holly saw him run his hands through his hair—a nervous gesture. "Can you just tell me why you came back?"

"To thank you for the flowers. Everyone on the island appreciated the gesture," she replied jovially, trying to ease her own nerves with a joke.

"I thought you would like it."

"I did," she told him hurriedly. "It showed that you listened."

"I always did," he said, looking down at his hands. "Even though I wasn't always good at showing it. I made a mistake and I am devoted to making it up to you every day for the rest of my life. Holly, I know I've said it before, but I truly mean it, I need you."

Holly put her drink on the nightstand and moved to the edge of the bed to be closer to him. He was so near; she could smell the sharp scent of his expensive cologne. "I need you, too. I just didn't expect to see such a terrible side of you that morning. It wasn't the man I knew."

"And it's *not* me," he said in such a torn voice, Holly was compelled to believe him. "Holly, I'll do anything to make you see how dedicated I am to you and our relationship, if I'm lucky enough for you to give me another shot. I'll end this campaign now and take some time off work. We can spend some time together, just us. We'll go anywhere you want."

"I can't let you do that," Holly told him. She knew how much he wanted to win and couldn't be the reason he failed at his venture. "This is what you've worked toward."

"But I will, for you. I'll do anything for you." He took her hands in his and pulled her to stand before him, pressing her fingers to his lips. "Holly, I love you."

She felt the room spin and her chest tighten with emotion. It was the moment she dreamed of, but she could barely bring herself to speak. "Jackson, I—"

"You don't need to tell me that you don't feel the same. Just know that I love you so much that I feel like I can't survive another day without you beside me. I wake up every morning cursing myself for being the reason you're not next to me. If you want to live in Michigan, just say the word and I'll operate Cantrell International from your island. I'll move the whole business and you can still work with your family, or not. Whatever you want to do. Just…please…give me another chance to show you that I can be the man you deserve. I don't want you to hate me."

Holly felt tears slip down her cheeks. "Jackson, you stupid idiot, I don't hate you. I couldn't even hate you when I actively tried. I love you, too."

She buried her face in his chest. It was all too good to be true. When she got on the plane the night before, Holly didn't have a plan. And, by the time she landed, her only determined course of action was to find Jackson. She was lucky that a stewardess recognized her behind the pair of large sunglasses she wore and politely asked if she was going to the rally. Going up on stage was a gamble, but one that she was glad she took.

Jackson pulled away slightly, kissing her softly on the lips. "Come on, Holly, let's go home."

Chapter Twenty-One

Jackson watched Holly put on her makeup in the bathroom mirror. She looked so perfect standing there, dressed in nothing more than her silk, leopard robe, her hair a golden river down her back and her legs, two smooth stalks below the hem. He knew he was a lucky man to have her back in his life.

Ursula knew it, too.

"My darling!" she shrieked when he and Holly came to the apartment after the rally, her bags under their arms.

"Hi, Ursula." Holly hugged her.

"I take it by the luggage you are here to stay?" Ursula asked hopefully, much in the same way Jackson had a few hours earlier. "Is the doorman bringing up the rest of your things?"

"I was planning to, but I left most of my stuff back in Michigan." Holly pointed to her two small suitcases. "But I still have more than enough to get by."

Ursula eyed the bags with distain. "Not even a single garment bag?"

"Mother," Jackson cut in. "She could only take so much on the plane. They usually allow you only one carry on."

"You mean you flew *commercial*?" Ursula had looked scandalized, turning on her son. "What is the meaning of this?"

"He didn't know I was coming," Holly said urgently. "I surprised him."

Ursula let out a deep breath. "Thank goodness. I had thought I raised a savage."

Holly beamed, taking Jackson's hand. "No, you raised a gentlemen.

Ursula had then smiled at him. "Now, my son, it seems you are a man."

***

Jackson came up behind Holly as she put her makeup back into a small bag, wrapping his arms around her waist. "You look gorgeous."

Holly giggled. "I'm not even dressed."

"All the better," he said, nipping at the exposed skin of her neck. They had been separated for two weeks, but it was the longest two weeks of his life and he craved her desperately.

"Shouldn't you be doing something productive? We're going to be late for the election results." Still, she smiled at his reflection before turning in his arms. "I have to get dressed, too."

"Do you really?" Jackson pulled at the tie on her robe but Holly swiftly slapped his hand away.

"No more funny business." She slipped out of the bathroom and into the closet where her meager items were now hung.

As Jackson picked his suit up from the bed, he made a mental note to plan for a shopping spree to replenish her abandoned clothes. He thought about jetting off to Paris to his the stores there, or just let her go wild with a private shopper. No matter what, Jackson knew he needed to be on his 'A' game. He had lost Holly once, and wasn't about to lose her again.

"Can you zip me up?" Holly stepped from the closet in a black dress, a trim of red-embroidered hem brushing her knees. She held a pair of red pumps in her hand and slipped one on after the other.

Jackson's breath hitched in his throat as she spun to allow him access to her back. He looked at the creamy skin of her shoulders and wondered if they *really* needed to go. Sure, it was his own party, but if he lost, he would regret going in the first place. However, he knew he wouldn't regret a few hours back in bed with Holly.

"Zip," she ordered, pointing at her neck. "Stop messing around."

"Fine." He fastened the dress and leaned in to place his lips upon her neck. "But, later you're mine."

***

The Manhattan Marriot's event space was draped in American flags and republican banners when they arrived to booming applause. Jackson held Holly's hand as they made their way through the throng of supporters, photographers, and reporters. By the time they made it to the front of the room, his hand was almost numb from all the firm handshakes he had to give.

"You're late," Denny grumbled as the pair joined him on the low stage.

"Traffic," Jackson said smoothly. "Denny, this is Holly. Holly, my manager, Denny."

"Great to meet you." Denny shook her hand enthusiastically.

"Great to meet you, too," Holly said, a timid smile on her lips.

Denny released her and pulled out his phone showing Jackson a number of pie charts and percentages. "Have you seen the current numbers?"

"Not a single digit."

"You're up to forty-one percent," Denny told him. "So far we're thinking you could really have a shot at winning this."

Jackson nodded, surprised. He glanced at Holly, who was chatting with a female reporter, and pondered if her return was the reason for his rising popularity. The public seemed to love her small-town charm almost as much as Jackson did. Either way, she was changing everything for the better.

"Go on, say a little something to greet your guests." Denny elbowed him. "Come on, give them some personality, don't just follow Holly around like a love-sick teenager all night."

Jackson chose to ignore the jab, and went up to the podium, silencing the crowd at once with a smile and a nod.

"Good evening, everyone," Jackson began.

"Thank you for joining me on this political journey and for giving me your support to be the Republican Mayor of New York City!" He paused as the group clapped and whistled. "You know my stances, my business strategies, my ideas for the city's growth. I want to work for you, *with* you, to make this city better, safer, cleaning, and healthier. I have big plans for New York and I hope I get the opportunity to set them into motion. Start the timer!"

A large, digital, screen above the stage turned on, showing 2:00 on the display. The number then changed to 1:59. The countdown to the closing off the polls and announcement of the election results had begun and Jackson couldn't believe his luck. Not only had Holly returned to him, but also he had the respect of his mother, the love of the city, and had a real shot at actually winning the election. It was like a scene from a movie—too good to be true.

"Penny for your thoughts?" Holly asked, handing him a champagne flute.

He looked down at her fondly, firmly thankful to share this moment with her. "Everything's just falling into place so well. I'm almost waiting for the other shoe to drop."

"The city loves you again and you've sufficiently groveled enough for me to no longer want to punch you in the face," Holly told him, daintily taking a sip from her champagne. "Relax a little. Everything's out of your hands now. Just be happy."

"I am," Jackson told her, cupping her face with his hand. "Trust me."

Holly gave him a small wave and an even smaller smile, urging him to join her. The reporters turned toward his place at the edge of the stage, the cameras clicking wildly.

Holly held out her hand as Jackson approached. "Are you going to help a girl up?"

He nodded, pulling up to her feet and immediately enveloping her into a tight embrace. "I don't care if you're here to destroy me to the presses, I'm just so goddamn happy to see you."

"If that's why you think I'm here, then you didn't learn a think about me and I made a mistake in coming," Holly whispered in his ear, sending a shiver down his spine.

"Never." He pulled back, looking into her upturned, heart shaped face, unable to recall a more breathtaking sight. "I can't believe you came back."

"All right, love birds, we get it! You love each other!" a voice called from the crowd. "Let's get it moving!"

"We'll talk later." Holly detached herself from him and stood a few steps away from the podium, looking every bit the part of a politician's wife.

The Non-Disclosure Agreement

***

Holly bit her lip, watching as the clock struck zero. Denny took out his cellphone to wait for the call. Jackson looked relaxed, now, and mingled freely with the guests while Holly stood back and observed. His carriage was vastly different than when he was in her hotel room. There he looked defeated and tired. But here, at his cocktail party, he was confident and stood tall as he spoke with people, smiling easily.

"Nervous?" Ursula appeared beside her, looking very much like Morticia Addams in a floor length dress that was so blue it was nearly black.

"A little. Jackson really wants this."

Ursula waved a hand. "Not this. You and him."

"A little," she responded with a light laugh. "But I think he's worth the gamble."

"I'm glad you think so." Ursula looked pleased as she scanned the crowd.

Holly was about to ask her how long she would stay in New York when Denny's phone let out a shrill screech. He fumbled with the screen and turned away from the crowd, speaking in a low tone before pocketing his cell and whispering something in Jackson's ear. Jackson nodded grimly and motioned for Holly to join him.

Holly's heart dropped. She hadn't planned on him losing the election and would hate for him to have to close the door on his political aspirations. She passed her glass to a waiter and joined him on the stage, taking his hand and squeezing it in reassurance. If he lost, as Holly suspected he had, then he was going to need all the love and support she could offer him.

"May I have your attention?" Jackson requested of the already rapt audience. "I would like to announce that…." He paused.

Holly's stomach did a flip and she held her breath as she waited for him to continue.

"I would like to announce that you are currently at a victory reception for the new Mayor of New York City!"

Holly let out an involuntary squeal of delight. "Congratulations!"

"I couldn't have done it without you," Jackson said over the crowd before turning back to the microphone. "Thank you all for your unwavering encouragement. Now, I'd like to reintroduce you to the beautiful woman at my side."

Holly felt her cheeks heat, not exactly welcoming the hundreds of eyes upon her. All she really wanted to do in that moment was take Jackson behind the curtain and show him the real perks of being mayor. But he looked too thrilled to be up there, basking in the glory of his win, that she couldn't even be irked at him calling her out.

"Holly McIntyre has been my constant rock throughout the last leg of my campaign and continues to be my beacon of hope in this world. I would never have been able to secure this mayoral position without her as my partner. She's my partner in politics, campaigning, and I want her to be my partner in life."

Holly furrowed her brow as Jackson turned to her, going down on one knee, his hand in his suit pocket. For a moment she thought back to the first time he was on his knees before her in his office, begging her to pretend to be his fiancée for the voters, and stifled a nervous laugh. "Jackson, what are you doing?"

"Holly, I love you," he began in a low voice, too quiet for the crowd to hear. "I've messed up in major ways, and somehow, you've decided to give me a second chance. You've been everything to me these past few months and I can't think of anything I'd want more than for you to continue on with me as my wife." He held out her engagement ring, taking her hand. "Marry me, Holly, and I promise that I will make you happy every day for the rest of your life."

Her mouth still hung open in shock as he looked from his eager face to the giant ring in his palm. "But everyone thinks we're already engaged."

"Screw everyone else. I only care what you think…and what you say now."

"Are you serious?"

"I've never been more serious in my entire life."

"And this is for real?"

"As real as this non-conflict diamond." He flashed her a cheeky grin. "Marry me, Holly."

"Do it!" Someone yelled, prompting the rest of the crowd to follow suit with a rousing. "Say yes, say yes!"

"Please, Holly." His icy eyes pleaded with her just as earnestly as his words.

"Yes," She whispered as he slid the band around her finger for the final time.

The pair then embraced to the enthusiastic cheers

of the supporters. Their lips locks and Holly gratefully felt the heavy ring weigh down her hand that was now clutching the back of her *real* fiancé's neck. And as the ceiling released colorful bursts of confetti and hundreds of victory balloons to the rousing delight of the crowd, Holly thought that maybe she had what it took to be a big city girl, after all.

Acknowledgments:

I'd like to give thanks to my editor, Rosa Sophia, who worked to bring this book to fruition.

About the Author

Kelsey McKnight is a university-educated historian from southern New Jersey. She has married her great loves of romance, history, and literature to create her newly finished works. *Queen of Emeralds*, published by Limitless Publishing, takes readers on a journey through the bustling streets of Victorian London and into the lush hills of the Scottish Highlands. When she's not working, Kelsey can be found reading, drinking too much coffee, spending time with her husband and daughter, and flitting around Twitter.

Twitter:
http://twitter.com/KelseyMMcK

Google Plus:
https://kelseymcknight.wordpress.com/

Goodreads:
http://kissatmidnight.wordpress.com/

Dedications:

This book is dedicated to "Seabass" who has, once again, sat through my numerous musings from beginning to end. And to fellow Limitless writer, Sarah Fischer, whose enthusiasm carried me through.